Stories to Tell a Six-Year-Old

Stories to Tell a Six-Year-Old

Selected by **Alice Low**

Illustrated by
Heather Harms Maione

Little, Brown and Company
BOSTON   NEW YORK   TORONTO   LONDON

For Sheila and Victor and their grandchildren:
Victoria, Lincoln, Alexandra, and Matthew
A. L.

Text compilation copyright © 1997 by Alice Low
Illustrations copyright © 1997 by Heather Harms Maione

First Edition

Copyright acknowledgments appear on page 183.

Library of Congress Cataloging-in-Publication Data

Stories to tell a six-year-old / selected by Alice Low ; illustrated by
Heather Harms Maione.—1st ed.
        p.   cm.
    Summary: Presents a collection of folk and fairy tales, contemporary
stories about everyday life, and excerpts from childhood classics.
    ISBN 0-316-53418-8
    1. Children's stories.   2. Tales.   [1. Short stories.   2. Fairy
tales.   3. Folklore.]   I. Low, Alice.   II. Maione, Heather Harms,
ill.
    PZ5.S88465   1996
    [E]—dc20
                                                    96-5387

10   9   8   7   6   5   4   3   2   1

MV- NY

Published simultaneously in Canada by Little, Brown & Company (Canada) Limited
Printed in the United States of America

CONTENTS

✦ Stories of Magic and Adventure ✦

The King's Toys   3
from Tick Tock Tales, *by Margaret Mahy*

Little Red-Cap   9
retold by Alice Low

The Scarecrow and the Tin Woodman   15
from Little Wizard Stories of Oz, *by L. Frank Baum*

The Practical Princess   24
by Jay Williams

The Ugly Duckling   36
adapted from Hans Christian Andersen

Pippi at the Circus   44
from Pippi Longstocking, *by Astrid Lindgren*

It Could Always Be Worse   55
retold by Margot Zemach

Laughing Gas   60
from Mary Poppins, *by P. L. Travers*

Talk   73
retold by Harold Courlander

v

The Big Cheese 78
by Miriam Schlein

The Wonderful Pearl 89
retold by James Riordan

✦ Stories of You and Me ✦

Two Big Bears 99
from Little House in the Big Woods, *by Laura Ingalls Wilder*

The Report Card 108
from Russell Sprouts, *by Johanna Hurwitz*

A Fruit and Vegetable Man 116
by Roni Schotter

Herbert's Treasure 123
by Alice Low

The Cat That Could Fly 130
by Joan Tarcher Durden

Rodeo Time 135
from Justin and the Best Biscuits in the World, *by Mildred Pitts Walter*

Henry and Ribs 141
from Henry Huggins, *by Beverly Cleary*

The Magic Shell *and* Making New Friends 155
from The Magic Shell, *by Nicholasa Mohr*

The Velveteen Rabbit, or How Toys Become Real   **167**
by Margery Williams

Acknowledgments   **183**

✦ Stories of ✦
Magic and Adventure

The King's Toys

by Margaret Mahy

What happens when a king who was never allowed to play with toys as a child finally gets the chance? Find out in this clever story from the book Tick Tock Tales.

When the king was just a little king, his mother, who was very strict, would not let him have any toys at all.

"You are a king," she said. "You must take life seriously. You must learn to spell."

His mother, the queen, thought that knowing how to spell was most important for a king. She had a room specially designed for him in which to practice his spelling.

When he was nearly a grown-up king, his mother left for a few days to visit her aunt who lived on top of a glass mountain. While his mother was away, the king decided to give himself a treat: He would buy a toy. By now he was the best speller of any monarch in the world, but in his entire life he had never had a single toy.

The king summoned the royal librarian. "Librarians are

meant to know everything," he said. "What toy would you suggest I buy?"

"Well, when I was small," said the librarian, "I used to be very fond of my teddy bear."

"Right!" said the king. So he sent his butler out to buy a teddy bear.

But the butler, who did not wish to be seen buying a toy, sent for a footman and told him to go instead.

But the footman did not want to be seen buying a teddy bear. So he sent for the page boy and told him to go in his place.

But the page boy, who was almost thirteen and very grown-up, did not want anyone to see him buying a teddy bear either. So he sent for the kitchen boy, Jack — the youngest of the king's staff.

Jack could scarcely believe his luck. He ran to the toy shop across the road from the palace and bought a beautiful, large golden teddy bear. He gave it to the page boy, who gave it to the footman, who gave it to the butler, who gave it to the king.

The king sat the bear on the mantelpiece in the royal spelling room.

"I like this bear," he said. "I like it so much that perhaps I should get another one. It will be rather lonely by itself."

"Why not try a rocking horse next?" suggested the librarian.

The king sent for the butler, who sent for the footman, who sent for the page boy, who sent for Jack. Jack chose a wonderful dapple-gray rocking horse with a long mane, an even longer tail, and a bridle hung all over with golden bells.

Now that the king had a teddy bear and a rocking horse, there was no stopping him. Jack was busy all day running across the road to the toy shop and then dashing back again with big packages tied with shiny ribbon. Every day was like Christmas for the king.

Jack chose a Noah's ark for him, and then a monkey on a stick, and a dollhouse — with tiny plants, a rocking chair, a pink cake on the kitchen table, as well as a dear little four-poster bed.

Jack bought a windup clown, building blocks, and a tin man in a checked coat who went *wibble-wobble, wibble-wobble* up and down a tin ladder. He chose hero dolls with bulging muscles, and robot dolls that obeyed orders, an electric train, and four racing cars.

The king's royal spelling room gradually became a royal toy room. Soon it was so full of toys that there wasn't room for any more.

"Right!" exclaimed the king. "That's enough. Now let's see what happens next."

The king sent for his golden throne (which two footmen trundled along the palace corridors to the royal spelling room) and sat down. He looked at his huge collection of toys, waiting for them to do something. He sat there, on and off, for three days — waiting expectantly. The teddy bear stared back at him, and so did the rocking horse. The dolls in the dollhouse, the hero dolls, the robot dolls, and the tin man in the checked coat all stared at the king,

and he stared back at them. Nobody did anything. At last, the king sent for the butler.

"I certainly have a lot of toys," he said.

"You do have a lovely collection, Your Majesty," agreed the butler.

"Yes, but when are they going to *do* something?" the king asked.

But the butler seemed to have forgotten exactly what toys were supposed to do.

"One moment," he said, and shot off through the maze of palace corridors to find the footman. "Just remind me," the butler said, "for it's a long time since I had any toys myself . . . what are the king's toys supposed to *do?*"

"Just remind me," the footman said, hurrying to the page boy. "What are those toys supposed to *do?*"

The page boy ran to the kitchen and found Jack scrubbing soup off a royal saucepan.

"The king has been waiting for his toys to *do* something," he cried. "They won't budge!"

"Why not let me talk to the king?" Jack suggested boldly. So the page boy took Jack to the footman, and the footman took him to the butler, and the butler took him to the king.

"His Majesty wishes to know when the toys are going to *do* something," the butler said sternly to Jack. Jack looked at the king. He looked at the toys.

"Your Majesty, *you* are the one who has to do something," Jack cried. "Toys are meant to be *played* with. They are waiting for you to *play* with them."

"Play?" cried the king. He spelled the word: "P-L-A-Y! But how do I P-L-A-Y?"

"I'll show you!" cried Jack. He grabbed the teddy bear and leaped onto the rocking horse. Then he rocked until the horse nearly came off its elegant rockers. He made the dollhouse dolls

ask the hero dolls and robot dolls to tea, and they all had a slice of pink cake, and yet there was plenty left over.

"I'm beginning to get the idea," said the king excitedly, seizing a green racing car. He put one of the hero dolls in the driving seat and set it off *brrroom-brrrooming* around the room, making tooting noises at every corner.

When the king's mother came back from her visit to the glass mountain, she realized her son would never be the same again. The king had appointed Jack his minister of play, and they played with the toys together every day — to keep in practice. And in return, the king taught Jack how to S-P-E-L-L, and even to R-E-A-D, and what could have been fairer than that?

Little Red-Cap

retold by Alice Low

Can Little Red-Cap outsmart the sneaky wolf? A fairy tale favorite adapted from the Brothers Grimm.

There was once a little girl much loved by everybody, but most of all by her grandmother, who could never do enough for the child. One day she gave her granddaughter a cap of red velvet, so bright and cheerful that it became the little girl's favorite hat. She wore it all the time, and that is why everyone, even her mother, called her Little Red-Cap.

On a sunny day in May, Little Red-Cap's mother said, "Come, Little Red-Cap, here is a basket with some cakes and a bottle of cider to take to your grandmother. She is ill and weak, and they will do her good. Go quickly now, before it gets too hot, and don't run, or you might fall and break the bottle or drop the cakes, and then your loving grandmother would have nothing. And stay on the path, and don't forget to say 'good morning' to your grandmother when you go into her room."

"I will be very careful," said Little Red-Cap, "and I will remember to do everything you have asked." And she set off with her precious basket.

Now, the grandmother lived in the woods about a mile from the village. Little Red-Cap stayed on the path, and just as she entered the woods, she met a wolf. However, she was not afraid, for she did not know that he was a wicked animal.

"Good day, Little Red-Cap," said he.

"Thank you kindly," answered she.

"Where are you going so early, Little Red-Cap?"

"To my grandmother's."

"What are you carrying in that basket?"

"Cakes and cider for my grandmother, who is ill and weak."

"Where does your grandmother live, Little Red-Cap?"

"Not too far from here," said Little Red-Cap. "Her house stands under the three oak trees, and there is a clump of hazel bushes in front of it. You must have seen it."

"That I have," said the wolf, thinking, The weak grandmother would be easier to catch, but this tender young thing would make a delicious meal and would taste even better. I must think of a way to get both of them.

Then he walked along with Little Red-Cap for a while and said, "Little Red-Cap, just look at the pretty flowers growing all around you, and listen to the sweet songs of the birds. You are hurrying along just as if you were going to school. Why not take your time and enjoy yourself? It is so delightful out here in the woods."

Little Red-Cap glanced around her, and when she saw the sunbeams darting here and there through the trees, and the lovely flowers everywhere, she said to herself, If I were to pick some flowers and make a bouquet for my grandmother, she would be very pleased. It is still early, and I shall get to her cottage in plenty of time.

And so she left the path and ran about in the woods, looking for the prettiest flowers. As soon as she had picked one, she saw a still prettier one a little farther away, and little by little, she went deeper and deeper into the woods.

But the wolf ran straight to the grandmother's house and knocked at the door.

"Who is there?" said the grandmother.

"Little Red-Cap," he answered, "and I have brought you some cake and cider. Please open the door."

"Lift the latch," cried the grandmother. "I am too weak to get up."

So the wolf lifted the latch, and the door flew open, and he fell on the grandmother and ate her up without saying one word. Then he put on her clothes and her nightcap, lay down in her bed, and drew the curtains.

11

All this time Little Red-Cap had been running here and there picking flowers, and when she had gathered as many as she could hold, she remembered her grandmother and set off for her cottage.

She was surprised to find the door wide open. When she went inside, she felt very strange, and she thought, Oh, dear, why do I feel so uneasy here when I usually love being at my grandmother's?

She called out, "Good morning," as she always did, but there was no answer. Then she went up to the bed and drew back the curtains. There lay her grandmother with her nightcap pulled over her eyes, so that she looked very odd and somehow different.

"Oh, Grandmother," she said, "what a big nose you have!"

"The better to smell you with" was the answer.

"Oh, Grandmother, what big eyes you have!" she said.

"The better to see you with, my child."

"Oh, Grandmother, what big hands you have!"

"The better to hug you with."

"But grandmother, what a terrible huge mouth you have!"

"The better to eat you with!"

And no sooner had the wolf said this than he bounded from the bed and swallowed up poor Little Red-Cap.

Then the wolf, having satisfied his hunger, lay down again in the bed and began to snore loudly.

Just then, a huntsman passed by and thought, How the grandmother snores! I had better see if there is anything the matter with her.

He went into the room, walked up to the bed, and saw the wolf lying there.

"At last I have found you, you old sinner!" he cried. "I have been looking for you for a long time."

He realized that the wolf had swallowed the grandmother whole, and he did not shoot, for she might yet be saved. He acted quickly, taking a pair of scissors and making snips in the wolf's stomach.

When he had made a few snips, he saw Little Red-Cap's head, and when he made a few more snips, Little Red-Cap jumped out, crying, "Oh, dear, how frightened I was! It was so dark inside the wolf."

And then out came the grandmother, still living and breathing!

Then Little Red-Cap had the idea to fill the wolf's belly with stones. And when the wolf woke up and started to rush away, the stones made him so heavy that he fell down dead.

Little Red-Cap and her grandmother and the huntsman danced around and cheered. The grandmother ate the cakes and drank the cider and felt strong and well again. And Little Red-Cap said to herself, I will never again wander off the path in the woods, but will walk straight to my grandmother's, just as my mother told me.

The Scarecrow and the Tin Woodman

by L. Frank Baum

Did you know that the Scarecrow and the Tin Woodman had many adventures after Dorothy left the Land of Oz? Read about one of them in this tale from The Little Wizard Stories of Oz.

There lived in the Land of Oz two queerly made men who were the best of friends. They were so much happier when together that they were seldom apart; yet they liked to separate, once in a while, that they might enjoy the pleasure of meeting again.

One was a Scarecrow. That means he was a suit of blue Munchkin clothes, stuffed with straw, on top of which was fastened a round cloth head, filled with bran to hold it in shape. On the head were painted two eyes, two ears, a nose, and a mouth. The Scarecrow had never been much of a success in scaring crows, but he prided himself on being a superior man, because he could feel no pain, was never tired, and did not have to eat or drink. His brains were sharp, for the Wizard of Oz had put pins and needles in the Scarecrow's brains.

The other man was made all of tin, his arms and legs and head being cleverly jointed so that he could move them freely. He was known as the Tin Woodman, having at one time been a woodchopper, and everyone loved him because the Wizard had given him an excellent heart of red plush.

The Tin Woodman lived in a magnificent tin castle, built on his country estate in the Winkie Land, not far from the Emerald City of Oz. It had pretty tin furniture and was surrounded by lovely gardens in which were many tin trees and beds of tin flowers. The palace of the Scarecrow was not far distant, on the banks of a river, and this palace was in the shape of an immense ear of corn.

One morning the Tin Woodman went to visit his friend the Scarecrow, and as they had nothing better to do, they decided to take a boat ride on the river. So they got into the Scarecrow's boat, which was formed from a big corncob, hollowed out and pointed at both ends and decorated around the edges with brilliant jewels. The sail was of purple silk and glittered gaily in the sunshine.

There was a good breeze that day, so the boat glided swiftly over the water. By and by they came to a smaller river that flowed from a deep forest, and the Tin Woodman proposed they sail up this stream, as it would be cool and shady beneath the trees of the forest. So the Scarecrow, who was steering, turned the boat up the stream, and the friends continued talking together of old times and the wonderful adventures they had met with while traveling with Dorothy, the little Kansas girl. They became so much interested in this talk that they forgot to notice that the boat was now sailing through the forest, or that the stream was growing more narrow and crooked.

Suddenly the Scarecrow glanced up and saw a big rock just ahead of them.

"Look out!" he cried, but the warning came too late.

The Tin Woodman sprang to his feet just as the boat bumped into the rock, and the jar made him lose his balance. He toppled and fell overboard, and being made of tin, he sank to the bottom of the water in an instant and lay there at full length, faceup.

Immediately the Scarecrow threw out the anchor, so as to hold the boat in that place, and then he leaned over the side and through the clear water looked at his friend sorrowfully.

"Dear me!" he exclaimed. "What a misfortune!"

"It is, indeed," replied the Tin Woodman, speaking in muffled tones because so much water covered him. "I cannot drown, of course, but I must lie here until you find a way to get me out. Meantime, the water is soaking into all my joints, and I shall become badly rusted before I am rescued."

"Very true," agreed the Scarecrow, "but be patient, my friend, and I'll dive down and get you. My straw will not rust and is easily replaced if damaged, so I'm not afraid of the water."

The Scarecrow now took off his hat and made a dive from the boat into the water. But his body was so light that he barely dented the surface of the stream, nor could he reach the Tin Woodman with his outstretched straw arms. So he floated to the boat and climbed into it, saying all the while, "Do not despair, my friend. We have an extra anchor aboard, and I will tie it around my waist, to make me sink, and dive again."

"Don't do that!" called the tin man. "That would anchor you also to the bottom, where I am, and we'd both be helpless."

"True enough," sighed the Scarecrow, wiping his wet face with a handkerchief; and then he gave a cry of astonishment, for he found he had wiped off one painted eye and now had but one eye to see with.

"How dreadful!" said the poor Scarecrow. "That eye must have been painted in watercolor, instead of oil. I must be careful not to wipe off the other eye, for then I could not see to help you at all."

A shriek of elfish laughter greeted this speech, and looking up, the Scarecrow found the trees full of black crows, who seemed much amused by the straw man's one-eyed countenance. He knew the crows well, however, and they had usually been friendly to him.

"Don't laugh," said he. "You may lose an eye yourselves someday."

"We couldn't look as funny as you, if we did," replied one old crow, the king of them. "But what has gone wrong with you?"

"The Tin Woodman, my dear friend and companion, has fallen overboard and is now on the bottom of the river," said the Scarecrow. "I'm trying to get him out again, but I fear I shall not succeed."

"Why, it's easy enough," declared the old crow. "Tie a string to him, and all of my crows will fly down, take hold of the string, and pull him up out of the water. There are hundreds of us here, so our united strength could lift much more than that."

"But I can't tie a string to him," replied the Scarecrow. "My straw is so light that I am unable to dive through the water. I've tried it, and knocked one eye out."

"Can't you fish for him?"

"Ah, that is a good idea," said the Scarecrow. "I'll make the attempt."

He found a fishline in the boat, with a stout hook at the end of it. No bait was needed, so the Scarecrow dropped the hook into the water till it touched the Woodman.

"Hook it into a joint," advised the crow, who was now perched upon a branch that stuck far out and bent down over the water.

The Scarecrow tried to do this, but having only one eye, he could not see the joints very clearly.

"Hurry up, please," begged the Tin Woodman. "You've no idea how damp it is down here."

"Can't you help?" asked the crow.

"How?" inquired the tin man.

"Catch the line and hook it around your neck."

The Tin Woodman made the attempt and after several trials wound the line around his neck and hooked it securely.

"Good!" cried the King Crow, a mischievous old fellow "Now, then, we'll all grab the line and pull you out."

At once the air was filled with black crows, each of whom seized the cord with beak or talons.

The Scarecrow watched them with much interest and forgot that he had tied the other end of the line around his own waist, so he would not lose it while fishing for his friend.

"All together for the good caws!" shrieked the King Crow, and with a great flapping of wings the birds rose into the air.

The Scarecrow clapped his stuffed hands in glee as he saw his friend drawn from the water into the air; but the next moment the straw man was himself in the air, his stuffed legs kicking wildly, for the crows had flown straight up through the trees. On one end of the line dangled the Tin Woodman, hung by the neck, and on the other dangled the Scarecrow, hung by the waist and clinging fast to the spare anchor of the boat, which he had seized hoping to save himself.

"Hi, there—be careful!" shouted the Scarecrow to the crows. "Don't take us so high. Land us on the riverbank."

But the crows were bent on mischief. They thought it a good joke to bother the two, now that they held them captive.

"Here's where the crows scare the Scarecrow!" cried the naughty King Crow, chuckling, and at his command the birds flew over the forest to where a tall dead tree stood higher than all the other trees. At the very top was a crotch, formed by two dead limbs, and into the crotch the crows dropped the center of the line. Then, letting go their hold, they flew away, chattering with laughter, and left the two friends suspended high in the air—one on each side of the tree.

Now, the Tin Woodman was much heavier than the Scarecrow, but the reason they balanced so nicely was because the straw man still clung fast to the iron anchor. There they hung, not ten feet apart, yet unable to reach the bare tree trunk.

"For goodness sake don't drop that anchor," said the Tin Woodman anxiously.

"Why not?" inquired the Scarecrow.

"If you did, I'd tumble to the ground, where my tin would be badly dented by the fall. Also you would shoot into the air and alight somewhere among the treetops."

"Then," said the Scarecrow earnestly, "I shall hold fast to the anchor."

For a time they both dangled in silence, the breeze swaying them gently to and fro. Finally the tin man said, "Here is an emergency, friend, where only brains can help us. We must think of some way to escape."

"I'll do the thinking," replied the Scarecrow. "My brains are the sharpest."

He thought so long that the tin man grew tired and tried to change his position, but found his joints had already rusted so badly that he could not move them. And his oilcan was back in the boat.

"Do you suppose your brains are rusted, friend Scarecrow?" he asked in a weak voice, for his jaws would scarcely move.

"No, indeed. Ah, here's an idea at last!"

And with this the Scarecrow clapped his hands to his head, forgetting the anchor, which tumbled to the ground. The result was astonishing, for, just as the tin man had said, the light

Scarecrow flew into the air, sailed over the top of the tree, and landed in a bramble-bush, while the tin man fell plump to the ground and, landing on a bed of dry leaves, was not dented at all. The Tin Woodman's joints were so rusted, however, that he was unable to move, while the thorns held the Scarecrow a fast prisoner.

While they were in this sad plight, the sound of hooves was heard, and along the forest path rode the little Wizard of Oz, seated on a wooden Sawhorse. He smiled when he saw the one-eyed head of the Scarecrow sticking out of the bramble-bush, but he helped the poor straw man out of his prison.

"Thank you, dear Wiz," said the grateful Scarecrow. "Now we must get the oilcan and rescue the Tin Woodman."

Together they ran to the riverbank, but the boat was floating in midstream and the Wizard was obliged to mumble some magic words to draw it to the bank, so the Scarecrow could get the oilcan. Then back they flew to the tin man, and while the Scarecrow carefully oiled each joint, the little Wizard moved the joints gently back and forth until they worked freely. After an hour of this labor, the Tin Woodman was again on his feet, and although still a little stiff, he managed to walk to the boat.

The Wizard and the Sawhorse also got aboard the corncob craft, and together they returned to the Scarecrow's palace. But the Tin Woodman was very careful not to stand up in the boat again.

The Practical Princess

by Jay Williams

Everyone's heard of beautiful princesses. But have you ever met a practical *one?*

Princess Bedelia was as lovely as the moon shining upon a lake full of water lilies. She was as graceful as a cat leaping. And she was also extremely practical.

When she was born, three fairies had come to her cradle to give her gifts, as was usual in that country. The first fairy had given her beauty. The second had given her grace. But the third, who was a wise old creature, had said, "I give her common sense."

"I don't think much of that gift," said King Ludwig, raising his eyebrows. "What good is common sense to a princess? All she needs is charm."

Nevertheless, when Bedelia was eighteen years old, something happened that made the king change his mind.

A dragon moved into the neighborhood. He settled in a dark cave on top of a mountain, and the first thing he did was to

24

send a message to the king. "I must have a princess to devour," the message said, "or I shall breathe out my fiery breath and destroy the kingdom."

Sadly, King Ludwig called together his councilors and read them the message.

"Perhaps," said the prime minister, "we had better advertise for a knight to slay the dragon. That is what is generally done in these cases."

"I'm afraid we haven't time," answered the king. "The dragon has given us only until tomorrow morning. There is no help for it. We shall have to send him the princess."

Princess Bedelia had come to the meeting because, as she said, she liked to mind her own business and this was certainly her business.

"Rubbish!" she said. "Dragons can't tell the difference between princesses and anyone else. Use your common sense. He's just asking for me because he's a snob."

"That may be so," said her father, "but if we don't send you along, he'll destroy the kingdom."

"Right!" said Bedelia. "I see I'll have to deal with this myself." She left the council chamber. She got the largest and gaudiest of her state robes and stuffed it with straw and tied it together with string. Into the center of the bundle she packed about a hundred pounds of gunpowder. She got two strong young men to carry it up the mountain for her. She stood in front of the dragon's cave and called, "Come out! Here's the princess!"

The dragon came blinking and peering out of the darkness. Seeing the bright robe covered with gold and silver embroidery, and hearing Bedelia's voice, he opened his mouth wide.

At once, at Bedelia's signal, the two young men swung the

robe and gave it a good heave, right down the dragon's throat. Bedelia threw herself flat on the ground, and the two young men ran.

As the gunpowder met the flames inside the dragon, there was a tremendous explosion.

Bedelia got up, dusting herself off. "Dragons," she said, "are not very bright."

She left the two young men sweeping up the pieces, and she went back to the castle to have her geography lesson.

The lesson that morning was local geography.

"Our kingdom, Arapathia, is bounded on the north by Istven," said the teacher. "Lord Garp, the ruler of Istven, is old, crafty, rich, and greedy."

At that very moment, Lord Garp of Istven was arriving at the

castle. Word of Bedelia's destruction of the dragon had reached him. "That girl," said he, "is just the wife for me." And he had come with a hundred finely dressed courtiers and many presents to ask King Ludwig for her hand.

The king sent for Bedelia. "My dear," he said, clearing his throat nervously, "just see who is here."

"I see. It's Lord Garp," said Bedelia. She turned to go.

"He wants to marry you," said the king.

Bedelia looked at Lord Garp. His face was like an old napkin, crumpled and wrinkled. It was covered with warts, as if someone had left crumbs on the napkin. He had only two teeth. Six long hairs grew from his chin, and none on his head. She felt like screaming.

However, she said, "I'm very flattered. Thank you, Lord Garp. Just let me talk to my father in private for a minute."

When they had retired to a small room behind the throne, Bedelia said to the king, "What will Lord Garp do if I refuse to marry him?"

"He is rich, greedy, and crafty," said the king unhappily. "He is also used to having his own way in everything. He will be insulted. He will probably declare war on us, and then there will be trouble."

"Very well," said Bedelia. "We must be practical."

She returned to the throne room. Smiling sweetly at Lord Garp, she said, "My lord, as you know, it is customary for a princess to set tasks for anyone who wishes to marry her. Surely you wouldn't like me to break the custom. And you are bold and powerful enough, I know, to perform any task."

"That is true," said Lord Garp smugly, stroking the six hairs on his chin. "Name your task."

"Bring me," said Bedelia, "a branch from the Jewel Tree of Paxis."

Lord Garp bowed, and off he went. "I think," said Bedelia to her father, "that we have seen the last of him. For Paxis is a thousand miles away, and the Jewel Tree is guarded by lions, serpents, and wolves."

But in two weeks, Lord Garp was back. With him he bore a chest, and from the chest he took a wonderful twig. Its bark was of rough gold. The leaves that grew from it were of fine silver. The twig was covered with blossoms, and each blossom had petals of mother-of-pearl and centers of sapphires, the color of the evening sky.

Bedelia's heart sank as she took the twig. But then she said to herself, Use your common sense, my girl! Lord Garp never traveled two thousand miles in two weeks, nor is he the man to fight his way through lions, serpents, and wolves.

She looked more carefully at the branch. Then she said, "My lord, you know that the Jewel Tree of Paxis is a living tree, although it is all made of jewels."

"Why, of course," said Lord Garp. "Everyone knows that."

"Well," said Bedelia, "then why is it that these blossoms have no scent?"

Lord Garp turned red.

"I think," Bedelia went on, "that this branch was made by the jewelers of Istven, who are the best in the world. Not very nice of you, my lord. Some people might even call it cheating."

Lord Garp shrugged. He was too old and rich to feel ashamed. But like many men used to having their own way, the more Bedelia refused him, the more he was determined to have her. "Never mind all that," he said. "Set me another task. This time, I swear I will perform it."

Bedelia sighed. "Very well. Then bring me a cloak made from the skins of the salamanders who live in the Volcano of Scoria."

Lord Garp bowed, and off he went. "The Volcano of Scoria," said Bedelia to her father, "is covered with red-hot lava. It burns steadily with great flames and pours out poisonous smoke so that no one can come within a mile of it."

"You have certainly profited by your geography lessons," said the king with admiration.

Nevertheless, in a week, Lord Garp was back. This time, he carried a cloak that shone and rippled with all the colors of fire. It was made of scaly skins, stitched together with fine golden wire. Each scale was red and orange and blue, like a tiny flame. Bedelia took the splendid cloak. She said to herself, use your head, miss! Lord Garp never climbed the red-hot slopes of the Volcano of Scoria.

A fire was burning in the fireplace of the throne room. Bedelia hurled the cloak into it. The skins blazed up in a flash, blackened, and fell to ashes.

Lord Garp's mouth fell open. Before he could speak, Bedelia said, "That cloak was a fake, my lord. The skins of salamanders who can live in the Volcano of Scoria wouldn't burn in a little fire like that one."

Lord Garp turned pale with anger. He hopped up and down, unable at first to do anything but splutter.

"Ub — ub — ub!" he cried. Then, controlling himself, he said, "So be it. If I can't have you, no one shall!"

He pointed a long, skinny finger at her. On the finger was a magic ring. At once, a great wind arose. It blew through the

throne room. It sent King Ludwig flying one way and his guards the other. Bedelia was picked up and whisked off through the air. When she could catch her breath and look about her, she found herself in a room at the top of a tower.

Bedelia peered out of the window. About the tower stretched an empty, barren plain. As she watched, a speck appeared in the distance. A plume of dust rose behind it. It drew nearer and became Lord Garp on horseback.

He rode to the tower and looked up at Bedelia. "Aha!" he croaked. "So you are safe and snug, are you? And will you marry me now?"

"Never," said Bedelia firmly.

"Then stay there until never comes," snarled Lord Garp. Away he rode.

For the next two days, Bedelia felt very sorry for herself. She sat wistfully by the window, looking out at the empty plain. When she was hungry, food appeared on the table. When she was tired, she lay down on the narrow cot and slept. Each day Lord Garp rode by and asked if she had changed her mind, and each day she refused him. Her only hope was that, as so often happens in old tales, a prince might come riding by who would rescue her.

But on the third day, she gave herself a shake. "Now, then, pull yourself together," she said sternly. "If you sit waiting for a prince to rescue you, you may sit here forever. Be practical! If there's any rescuing to be done, you're going to have to do it yourself."

She jumped up. There was something she had not yet done, and now she did it. She tried the door.

It opened.

Outside were three other doors. But there was no sign of a stair, or any way down from the top of the tower. She opened two of the doors and found that they led into cells just like hers, but empty. Behind the last door, however, lay what appeared to be a haystack. From beneath it came the sound of snores. And between snores, a voice said, "Six million and twelve . . . *snore* . . . six million and thirteen . . . *snore* . . . six million and fourteen . . ."

Cautiously, she went closer. Then she saw that what she had taken for a haystack was in fact an immense pile of blond hair. Parting it, she found a young man, sound asleep.

As she stared, he opened his eyes. He blinked at her. "Who—?" he said. Then he said, "Six million and fifteen," closed his eyes, and fell asleep again.

Bedelia took him by the shoulder and shook him hard. He awoke, yawning, and tried to sit up. But the mass of hair made this difficult.

"What on earth is the matter with you?" Bedelia asked. "Who are you?"

"I am Prince Perian," he replied, "the rightful ruler of— oh, dear, here I go again. Six million and . . ." His eyes began to close.

Bedelia shook him again. He made a violent effort and managed to wake up enough to continue, "— of Istven. But Lord Garp has put me under a spell. I have to count sheep jumping over a fence, and this puts me to slee—ee—ee—" He began to snore lightly.

"Dear me," said Bedelia. "I must do something."

She thought hard. Then she pinched Perian's ear, and this woke him with a start.

"Listen," she said. "It's quite simple. It's all in your mind, you see. You are imagining the sheep jumping over the fence. No! Don't go to sleep again!

"This is what you must do. Imagine them jumping backward. As you do, *count* them backward, and when you get to *one,* you'll be wide awake."

The prince's eyes snapped open. "Marvelous!" he said. "Will it work?"

"It's bound to," said Bedelia. "If the sheep going one way will put you to sleep, their going back again will wake you up."

Hastily the prince began to count, "Six million and fourteen, six million and thirteen, six million and twelve . . ."

"Oh, my goodness," cried Bedelia, "count by hundreds, or you'll never get there."

He began to gabble as fast as he could, and with each moment that passed, his eyes sparkled more brightly, his face grew livelier, and he seemed a little stronger, until at last he shouted, "Five, four, three, two, ONE!" and awoke completely.

He struggled to his feet, with a little help from Bedelia.

"Heavens!" he said. "Look how my hair and beard have grown. I've been here for years. Thank you, my dear. Who are you, and what are you doing here?"

Bedelia quickly explained.

Perian shook his head. "One more crime of Lord Garp's," he said. "We must escape and see that he is punished."

"Easier said than done," Bedelia replied. "There is no stair in this tower, as far as I can tell, and the outside wall is much too smooth to climb down."

Perian frowned. "This will take some thought," he said. "What we need is a long rope."

"Use your common sense," said Bedelia. "We haven't any rope."

Then her face lit up, and she clapped her hands. "But we have your beard." She laughed.

Perian understood at once, and chuckled. "I'm sure it will reach almost to the ground," he said. "But we haven't any scissors to cut it off with."

"That is so," said Bedelia. "Hang it out of the window and let me climb down. I'll search the tower and perhaps I can find a ladder or a hidden stair. If all else fails, I can go for help."

She and the prince gathered up great armfuls of the beard and staggered into Bedelia's room, which had the largest window. The prince's long hair trailed behind and nearly tripped him. Perian threw the beard out of the window and braced himself, holding the beard with both hands to ease the pull on his chin. Bedelia climbed out of the window and slid down the beard.

But suddenly, out of the wilderness came the drumming of hooves, a cloud of dust, and then Lord Garp on his swift horse. With one glance, he saw what was happening. He shook his fist up at Prince Perian.

"Meddlesome fool!" he shouted. "I'll teach you to interfere."

He leaped from the horse and grabbed the beard. He gave it a tremendous yank. Headfirst came Perian, out of the window. Down he fell, and with a thump, he landed right on top of old Lord Garp.

This saved Perian, who was not hurt at all. But it was the end of Lord Garp.

Perian and Bedelia rode back to Istven on Lord Garp's horse.

In the great city, the prince was greeted with cheers of joy — once everyone had recognized him after so many years and under so much hair.

And of course, since Bedelia had rescued him from captivity, she married him. First, however, she made him get a haircut and a shave so that she could see what he really looked like. For she was always practical.

The Ugly Duckling

adapted from Hans Christian Andersen

*Have you ever felt that you just
didn't fit in, no matter how hard you
tried? Then you'll know how the
ugly duckling feels. . . .*

It was summer in the country. By the river a duck had built herself a warm nest and was sitting all day on six eggs. Five of them were white, but the sixth, which was larger than the others, was an ugly gray.

The duck sat on the nest for many days, until, at long last, the eggs began to crack, one after another. Soon five white eggs lay empty, and five pairs of duckling eyes gazed out upon the green world.

"Well, now, I hope you're all here," said the mother duck, and she got up to have a look. But the big gray egg had not hatched.

"I can't think what is the matter with it," the duck grumbled to an older duck who had come to pay a visit.

"Let me look at it," said the old neighbor. "Ah, I thought so.

It's a turkey egg, not a duck egg! Once, when I was young, I was tricked into sitting on a brood of turkey eggs myself. You should leave that gray egg where it is and teach the rest of your ducklings to swim."

"Well, let me sit on it a bit longer," said the duck.

"Please yourself," said the old duck, and waddled off.

At long last the big gray egg began to crack, and soon a big, awkward bird tumbled out. There was no denying that the chick was ugly. Could he really be a turkey? wondered the mother duck. But when she took her babies in for a swim, the ugly one swam just as well as his brothers and sisters, even if he was not half so pretty.

"*Quack! Quack!* Come along, children, and I'll introduce you to the other birds," said the mother duck. "Keep close, and watch out for the cat!"

The ducklings followed their mother into the poultry yard. The birds there said to themselves, "Oh, dear me, how many chicks! The yard is so full already! And did you ever see anything quite as ugly as that great tall one? Let's chase him out!"

And one duck ran up to the ugly duckling and nipped him on the neck.

"Leave him alone," cried his mother. "He was not troubling you."

But from that day onward, the other birds teased the ugly duckling whenever his mother was not looking. Even the turkey, who was ever so big, never passed without mocking him. And his brothers and sisters soon became as rude and unkind as the rest.

At last the ugly duckling could bear it no longer. One night, after all the ducks and hens had fallen asleep, he ran away. He scrambled down the bank of the river until he reached a grassy marsh where the wild ducks and geese lived. There he lay down, exhausted. But he was too frightened to sleep. For two days, he lay quietly among the reeds. He wished he could stay there forever, with nobody to bite him and tell him how ugly he was.

But the next morning, two wild geese appeared. "Listen," they said, after they had looked him over. "You're so ugly that we rather like you. Why not fly with us?"

Before the duckling could reply, loud shots rang out — *Bang! Bang!* — and the two geese fell down dead in front of him. The other wild ducks and geese took to the air, but the duckling, who could not fly, hid himself among some tall ferns. Suddenly an enormous dog stood in front of him. Its eyes glistened, and its long red tongue hung out of its mouth. The duckling grew cold with terror and tried to hide his head beneath his wings. But the dog just snuffled at him and passed by.

"I am even too ugly for a dog to eat," cried the ugly duckling.

At last all was quiet. With only the stars left to see him, the ugly duckling crept out and walked on until he reached a tumbledown cottage with a door hung upon only one hinge. Cautiously he edged by the door and lay down under a chair by the tiny fire.

Now, in the cottage lived an old woman, her cat, and a hen. The next morning, when they saw their visitor, the cat began to purr and the hen began to cluck. "What's the matter?" asked the old woman, looking around. But her eyesight was so poor that she mistook the young duckling for a full-grown duck. "What luck! Now we'll have duck eggs—that is, as long as it's not a drake! Well, we'll soon see."

And so the duckling stayed in the cottage with the woman and the hen and the cat for three weeks; but he laid no eggs.

The cat was master of the house, and the hen the mistress, and they thought very highly of themselves.

"Can you lay an egg, as I can?" the hen asked. And when the duck shook his head no, she turned her back on him.

"Can you ruffle your fur when you are angry or purr when you are pleased, as I can?" asked the cat. And again, the duckling had to admit that he could do nothing but swim, which did not seem to be of much use in the cottage.

The ugly duckling sat in a corner, feeling downhearted. Then, all at once, he remembered the fresh air and sunshine, and wanted with all his might to have a swim. At last, he couldn't resist telling the hen about it.

"I don't think I should enjoy swimming," replied the hen doubtfully. "And I don't think the cat would like it, either." And the cat, when asked, agreed that there was nothing she would hate more.

But the duckling couldn't stop thinking about the water. "I think I'll go out and look for a place to swim," he told them.

"All right, go," they answered, and turned away.

The duckling was sad to leave the cottage, but could not help feeling a thrill of joy when he was out on the water once more. He floated, and dived below the surface, and for a while was quite happy. But he soon saw that all the other ducks he met ignored him because he was so ugly.

Autumn came, and the leaves on the trees turned yellow and brown. One evening, as the sky was lit with a scarlet sunset, the duckling heard a sound of whirring wings. A flock of the most beautiful birds he had ever seen flew high up in the air above him. They were swans — as white as the snow that had fallen during the night. Their long necks and yellow bills stretched southward, for they were going to a land where the sun shone all day.

He had no idea what the birds were called or where they were from, but he was drawn to them as he had never been drawn to anything before. Oh, if only he could have gone with them! But what sort of companion could an ugly thing like him be for those beautiful creatures?

Every morning it grew colder and colder, and the ugly duckling had hard work keeping himself warm. At last, after one bitter night, his legs moved so slowly that the ice crept closer and closer, and when the morning light broke, he was caught fast.

But, by good fortune, a man crossing the river saw what had happened. He stamped on the ice so hard that it broke. Then, he picked up the duckling and tucked him under his coat, where the bird began to thaw a little. The man carried the ugly duckling home to his children, who gave him warm food and put him in a box by the fire. They were kind and wanted to play with him. But the poor duckling had never played in his life and thought they wanted to tease him, just like the ducks in the poultry yard. He flew straight into the milk pan, and then into the butter dish, and then, terrified by the noise and confusion, he flew right out the door and hid himself in the snow.

It would be too sad to tell of the misery and hardship that the ugly duckling had to face the rest of that winter. But before long the sun grew hotter, birds began to sing, and flowers bloomed once again.

The ugly duckling felt different, somehow, from how he had felt before. He lifted his wings, and they were stronger, and larger, and bore him easily. How glorious it felt to be rushing through the air! Before he knew it, he found himself in a garden where the apple trees blossomed and lilacs hung down over a long, winding stream. And then, from a thicket straight in front of him came three lovely swans, ruffling their wings and floating so lightly over the water. The duckling recognized the lovely birds, and a strange sadness came over him.

"I will fly over to these noble birds, even if they peck me to death for daring to go near them, ugly bird that I am! But I don't care — better to be killed by them than teased by ducks and hens, or to suffer through another winter!" And so he flew into the water and swam toward the splendid swans. They saw him, and rushed toward him, ruffling their feathers.

"Yes, kill me!" the ugly duckling cried. "I don't know why I was ever hatched, for I am too ugly to live!" And as he spoke, he bowed his head and looked down into the water. Yet what did he see? His own reflection — but it was no longer that of a dull, gray, ugly bird. Instead, he beheld a beautiful white swan!

"The new one is the best of all," cried the children when they came down to feed the swans before going to bed. "His feathers are whiter and his beak more golden than the rest!" And the other swans bowed before him.

It all made him feel quite bashful, and he tucked his head under his wing. But inside, he rejoiced with all his heart, and thought, I never dreamed of so much happiness when I was only an ugly duckling!

Pippi at the Circus

by Astrid Lindgren

A rollicking circus adventure from
Pippi Longstocking, *the first in the*
series of books featuring one of the
spunkiest girls ever.

A circus had come to the little town, and all the children were begging their mothers and fathers for permission to go. Of course Tommy and Annika asked to go, too, and their kind father immediately gave them some money.

Clutching it tightly in their hands, they rushed over to Pippi's. She was on the porch with her horse, braiding his tail into tiny pigtails and tying each one with red ribbon.

"I think it's his birthday today," she announced, "so he has to be all dressed up."

"Pippi," said Tommy, all out of breath because they had been running so fast, "Pippi, do you want to go with us to the circus?"

"I can go with you most anywhere," answered Pippi, "but whether I can go to the surkus or not I don't know, because I don't know what a surkus is. Does it hurt?"

"Silly!" said Tommy. "Of course it doesn't hurt; it's fun. Horses and clowns and pretty ladies that walk the tightrope."

"But it costs money," said Annika, opening her small fist to see if the shiny half-dollar and the quarters were still there.

"I'm rich as a troll," said Pippi, "so I guess I can buy a surkus all right. But it'll be crowded here if I have more horses. The clowns and the pretty ladies I could keep in the laundry, but it's harder to know what to do with the horses."

"Oh, don't be so silly," said Tommy. "You don't buy a circus. It costs money to go and look at it — see?"

"Preserve us!" cried Pippi, and shut her eyes tightly. "It costs money to *look?* And here I go around goggling all day long. Goodness knows how much money I've goggled up already!"

Then, little by little, she opened one eye very carefully, and it rolled round and round in her head. "Cost what it may," she said, "I must take a look!"

At last Tommy and Annika managed to explain to Pippi what a circus really was, and she took some gold pieces out of her suitcase. Then she put on her hat, which was as big as a millstone, and off they all went.

There were crowds of people outside the circus tent and a long line at the ticket window. But at last it was Pippi's turn. She stuck her head through the window and stared at the dear old lady sitting there.

"How much does it cost to look at you?" Pippi asked.

But the old lady was a foreigner who did not understand what Pippi meant and answered in broken Swedish.

"Little girl, it costs a dollar and a quarter in the grandstand and seventy-five cents on the benches and twenty-five cents for standing room."

Now Tommy interrupted and said that Pippi wanted a seventy-five-cent ticket. Pippi put down a gold piece, and the old lady looked suspiciously at it. She bit it, too, to see if it was genuine. At last she was convinced that it really was gold and gave Pippi her ticket and a great deal of change in silver.

"What would I do with all those nasty little white coins?" asked Pippi disgustedly. "Keep them, and then I can look at you twice. In the standing room."

As Pippi absolutely refused to accept any change, the lady changed her ticket to one for the grandstand and gave Tommy and Annika grandstand tickets, too, without their having to pay a single penny. In that way Pippi, Tommy, and Annika came to sit on some beautiful red chairs right next to the ring. Tommy and Annika turned around several times to wave to their schoolmates, who were sitting much farther away.

"This is a remarkable place," said Pippi, looking around in astonishment. "But, see, they've spilled sawdust all over the floor! Not that I'm overfussy myself, but that does look careless to me."

Tommy explained that all circuses had sawdust on the floor for the horses to run around in.

On a platform nearby, the circus band suddenly began to play a thundering march. Pippi clapped her hands wildly and jumped up and down with delight.

"Does it cost money to hear, too?" she asked. "Or can you do that for nothing?"

At that moment the curtain in front of the performers' entrance was drawn aside, and the ringmaster in a black frock coat, with a whip in his hand, came running in, followed by ten white horses with red plumes on their heads.

The ringmaster cracked his whip, and all the horses galloped around the ring. Then he cracked it again, and all the horses stood still with their front feet up on the railing around the ring.

One of them had stopped directly in front of the children. Annika didn't like to have a horse so near her and drew back in her chair as far as she could, but Pippi leaned forward and took the horse's right foot in her hands.

"Hello, there," she said, "my horse sent you his best wishes. It's his birthday today, too, but he has bows on his tail instead of on his head."

Luckily she dropped the foot before the ringmaster cracked his whip again, because then all the horses jumped away from the railing and began to run around the ring.

When the act was over, the ringmaster bowed politely and the horses ran out. In an instant the curtain opened again for a coal-black horse. On its back stood a beautiful lady dressed in green silk tights. The program said her name was Miss Carmencita.

The horse trotted around in the sawdust, and Miss Carmencita stood calmly on his back and smiled. But then something happened; just as the horse passed Pippi's seat, something came swishing through the air—and it was none other than Pippi herself. And there she stood on the horse's back, behind Miss Carmencita. At first Miss Carmencita was so astonished that she nearly fell off the horse. Then she got mad. She began to strike out with her hands behind her back to make Pippi jump off. But that didn't work.

"Take it easy," said Pippi. "Do you think you're the only one who can have any fun? Other people have paid, too, haven't they?"

Then Miss Carmencita tried to jump off herself, but that didn't work either, because Pippi was holding her tightly around the waist. At that the audience couldn't help laughing. They thought it was funny to see the lovely Miss Carmencita held against her will by a little redheaded youngster who stood there on the horse's back in her enormous shoes and looked as if she had never done anything except perform in a circus.

But the ringmaster didn't laugh. He turned toward an attendant in a red uniform and made a sign to him to go and stop the horse.

"Is this act already over," asked Pippi in a disappointed tone, "just when we were having so much fun?"

"Horrible child!" hissed the ringmaster between his teeth. "Get out of here!"

Pippi looked at him sadly. "Why are you mad at me?" she

asked. "What's the matter? I thought we were here to have fun."

She skipped off her horse and went back to her seat. But now two huge guards came to throw her out. They took hold of her and tried to lift her up.

They couldn't do it. Pippi sat absolutely still, and it was impossible to budge her although they tried as hard as they could. At last they shrugged their shoulders and went off.

Meanwhile the next act had begun. It was Miss Elvira about to walk the tightrope. She wore a pink tulle skirt and carried a pink parasol in her hand. With delicate little steps she ran out on the rope. She swung her legs gracefully in the air and did all sorts of tricks. It looked so pretty. She even showed how she could walk backward on the narrow rope. But when she got back to the little platform at the end of the rope, there stood Pippi.

"What are you going to do now?" asked Pippi, delighted when she saw how astonished Miss Elvira looked.

Miss Elvira said nothing at all but jumped down from the rope and threw her arms around the ringmaster's neck, for he was her father. And the ringmaster once more sent for his guards to throw Pippi out. This time he sent for five of them, but all the people shouted, "Let her stay! We want to see the redheaded girl." And they stamped their feet and clapped their hands.

Pippi ran out on the rope, and Miss Elvira's tricks were as nothing compared with Pippi's. When she got to the middle of the rope she stretched one leg straight up in the air, and her big shoe spread out like a roof over her head. She bent her foot a little so that she could tickle herself with it back of her ear.

The ringmaster was not at all pleased to have Pippi perform-
ing in his circus. He wanted to get rid of her, and so he stole up
and loosened the mechanism that held the rope taut, thinking
surely Pippi would fall down.

But Pippi didn't. She set the rope a-swinging instead. Back
and forth it swayed, and Pippi swung faster and faster, until suddenly she leaped out into the air and landed right on the ringmaster. He was so frightened he began to run.

"Oh, what a jolly horse!" cried Pippi. "But why don't you
have any pompoms in your hair?"

Now Pippi decided it was time to go back to Tommy and
Annika. She jumped off the ringmaster and went back to her
seat. The next act was about to begin, but there was a brief

pause because the ringmaster had to go out and get a drink of water and comb his hair.

Then he came in again, bowed to the audience, and said, "Ladies and gentlemen, in a moment you will be privileged to see the Greatest Marvel of all time, the Strongest Man in the World, the Mighty Adolf, whom no one has yet been able to conquer. Here he comes, ladies and gentlemen. Allow me to present to you THE MIGHTY ADOLF."

And into the ring stepped a man who looked as big as a giant. He wore flesh-colored tights and had a leopard skin draped around his stomach. He bowed to the audience and looked very pleased with himself.

"Look at these muscles," said the ringmaster, and squeezed the Mighty Adolf's arm where the muscles stood out like balls under the skin.

"And now, ladies and gentlemen, I have a very special invitation for you. Who will challenge the Mighty Adolf in a wrestling match? Which of you dares to try his strength against the World's Strongest Man? A hundred dollars for anyone who can conquer the Mighty Adolf! A hundred dollars, ladies and gentlemen! Think of that! Who will be the first to try?"

Nobody came forth.

"What did he say?" asked Pippi.

"He says that anybody who can lick that big man will get a hundred dollars," answered Tommy.

"I can," said Pippi, "but I think it would be too bad to, because he looks nice."

"Oh, no, you couldn't," said Annika, "he's the strongest man in the world."

"*Man,* yes," said Pippi, "but I am the strongest *girl* in the world—remember that."

51

Meanwhile the Mighty Adolf was lifting heavy iron weights and bending thick iron rods in the middle just to show how strong he was.

"Oh, come now, ladies and gentlemen," cried the ringmaster, "is there really nobody here who wants to earn a hundred dollars? Shall I really be forced to keep this myself?" And he waved a bill in the air.

"No, that you certainly won't be forced to do," said Pippi, and stepped over the railing into the ring.

The ringmaster was absolutely wild when he saw her. "Get out of here! I don't want to see any more of you," he hissed.

"Why do you always have to be so unfriendly?" said Pippi reproachfully. "I just want to fight with Mighty Adolf."

"This is no place for jokes," said the ringmaster. "Get out of here before the Mighty Adolf hears your impudent nonsense."

But Pippi went right by the ringmaster and up to Mighty Adolf. She took his hand and shook it heartily.

"Shall we fight a little, you and I?" she asked.

Mighty Adolf looked at her but didn't understand a word.

"In one minute I'll begin," said Pippi.

And begin she did. She grabbed Mighty Adolf around the waist, and before anyone knew what was happening she had thrown him on the mat. Mighty Adolf leaped up, his face absolutely scarlet.

"Atta girl, Pippi!" shrieked Tommy and Annika, so loudly that all the people at the circus heard it and began to shriek, "Atta girl, Pippi!" too. The ringmaster sat on the railing, wringing his hands. He was mad, but Mighty Adolf was madder. Never in his life had he experienced anything so humiliating as this. And he certainly intended to show that redheaded girl what kind of man Mighty Adolf really was. He rushed at Pippi and caught her round the waist, but Pippi stood firm as a rock.

"You can do better than that," she said to encourage him. Then she wriggled out of his grasp, and in the twinkling of an eye Mighty Adolf was on the mat again. Pippi stood beside him, waiting. She didn't have to wait long. With a roar he was up again, rushing at her.

"Tiddelipom and piddeliday," said Pippi.

All the people in the tent stamped their feet and threw their hats in the air and shouted, "Hurrah, Pippi!"

When Mighty Adolf came rushing at her for the third time, Pippi lifted him high in the air and, with her arms straight above her, carried him clear round the ring. Then she laid him down on the mat again and held him there.

"Now, little fellow," said she, "I don't think we'll bother about this anymore. We'll never have any more fun than we've had already."

"Pippi is the winner! Pippi is the winner!" cried all the people.

Mighty Adolf stole out as fast as he could, and the ringmaster had to go up and hand Pippi the hundred dollars, although he looked as if he'd much prefer to eat her.

"Here you are, young lady, here you are," he said. "One hundred dollars."

"That thing!" said Pippi scornfully. "What would I want with that old piece of paper. Take it and use it to fry herring on if you want to." And she went back to her seat.

"This is certainly a long surkus," she said to Tommy and Annika. "I think I'll take a little snooze, but wake me if they need my help with anything else."

And then she lay back in her chair and went to sleep at once. There she lay and snored while the clowns, the sword swallowers, and the snake charmers did their tricks for Tommy and Annika and all the rest of the people at the circus.

"Just the same, I think Pippi was best of all," whispered Tommy to Annika.

It Could Always Be Worse

retold by Margot Zemach

A clever rabbi teaches a man and his large family a lesson they won't soon forget in this hilarious retelling of a traditional Yiddish folktale.

Once upon a time in a small village a poor unfortunate man lived with his mother, his wife, and his six children in a little one-room hut. Because they were so crowded, the man and his wife often argued. The children were noisy, and they fought. In winter, when the nights were long and the days were cold, life was especially hard. The hut was full of crying and quarreling. One day, when the poor unfortunate man couldn't stand it anymore, he ran to the Rabbi for advice.

"Holy Rabbi," he cried, "things are in a bad way with me, and getting worse. We are so poor that my mother, my wife, my six children, and I all live together in one small hut. We are too crowded, and there's so much noise. Help me, Rabbi. I'll do whatever you say."

The Rabbi thought and pulled on his beard. At last he said,

"Tell me, my poor man, do you have any animals, perhaps a chicken or two?"

"Yes," said the man. "I do have a few chickens, also a rooster and a goose."

"Ah, fine," said the Rabbi. "Now, go home and take the chickens, the rooster, and the goose into your hut to live with you."

"Yes indeed, Rabbi," said the man, though he was a bit surprised.

The poor unfortunate man hurried home and took the chickens, the rooster, and the goose out of the shed and into his little hut.

When some days or a week had gone by, life in the hut was worse than before. Now with the quarreling and crying there was honking, crowing, and clucking. There were feathers in the soup. The hut stayed just as small and the children grew bigger.

When the poor unfortunate man couldn't stand it any longer, he again ran to the Rabbi for help.

"Holy Rabbi," he cried, "see what a misfortune has befallen me. Now with the crying and quarreling, with the honking, clucking, and crowing, there are feathers in the soup. Rabbi, it couldn't be worse. Help me, please."

The Rabbi listened and thought. At last he said, "Tell me, do you happen to have a goat?"

"Oh, yes, I do have an old goat, but he's not worth much."

"Excellent," said the Rabbi. "Now, go home and take the old goat into your hut to live with you."

"Ah, no! Do you really mean it, Rabbi?" cried the man.

"Come, come now, my good man, and do as I say at once," said the Rabbi.

The poor unfortunate man tramped back home with his head hanging down and took the old goat into his hut.

When some days or a week had gone by, life in the little hut was much worse. Now, with the crying, quarreling, clucking, honking, and crowing, the goat went wild, pushing and butting everyone with his horns. The hut seemed smaller; the children grew bigger.

When the poor unfortunate man couldn't stand it another minute, he again ran to the Rabbi.

"Holy Rabbi, help me!" he screamed. "Now the goat is running wild. My life is a nightmare."

The Rabbi listened and thought. At last he said, "Tell me, my poor man. Is it possible that you have a cow? Young or old doesn't matter."

"Yes, Rabbi, it's true I have a cow," said the poor man fearfully.

"Go home, then," said the Rabbi, "and take the cow into your hut."

"Oh, no, surely not, Rabbi!" cried the man.

"Do it at once," said the Rabbi.

The poor unfortunate man trudged home with a heavy heart and took the cow into his hut. Is the Rabbi crazy? he thought.

When some days or a week had gone by, life in the hut was very much worse than before. Everyone quarreled, even the chickens. The goat ran wild. The cow trampled everything. The poor man could hardly believe his misfortune. At last, when he could stand it no longer, he ran to the Rabbi for help.

"Holy Rabbi," he shrieked, "help me, save me, the end of the world has come! The cow is trampling everything. There is no room even to breathe. It's worse than a nightmare!"

The Rabbi listened and thought. At last he said, "Go home

now, my poor unfortunate man, and let the animals out of your hut."

"I will, I will, I'll do it right away," said the man.

The poor unfortunate man hurried home and let the cow, the goat, the chickens, the goose, and the rooster out of his little hut.

That night the poor man and all his family slept peacefully. There was no crowing, no clucking, no honking. There was plenty of room to breathe.

The very next day the poor man ran back to the Rabbi.

"Holy Rabbi," he cried, "you have made life sweet for me. With just my family in the hut, it's so quiet, so roomy, so peaceful. . . . What a pleasure!"

Laughing Gas

by P. L. Travers

*Mary Poppins can turn an ordinary
tea party into an extraordinary
adventure. Read all about it in this
story from* Mary Poppins, *the first
book in the classic series about a stern
but magical English nanny.*

"Are you quite sure he will be at home?" said Jane, as they got off the Bus, she and Michael and Mary Poppins.

"Would my uncle ask me to bring you to tea if he intended to go out, I'd like to know?" said Mary Poppins, who was evidently very offended by the question. She was wearing her blue coat with the silver buttons and the blue hat to match, and on the days when she wore these it was the easiest thing in the world to offend her.

All three of them were on the way to pay a visit to Mary Poppins's uncle, Mr. Wigg, and Jane and Michael had looked forward to the trip for so long that they were more than half afraid that Mr. Wigg might not be in, after all.

"Why is he called Mr. Wigg—does he wear one?" asked Michael, hurrying along beside Mary Poppins.

"He is called Mr. Wigg because Mr. Wigg is his name. And

he doesn't wear one. He is bald," said Mary Poppins. "And if I have any more questions we will just go Back Home." And she sniffed her usual sniff of displeasure.

Jane and Michael looked at each other and frowned. And the frown meant: "Don't let's ask her anything else or we'll never get there."

Mary Poppins put her hat straight at the Tobacconist's Shop at the corner. It had one of those curious windows where there seem to be three of you instead of one, so that if you look long enough at them you begin to feel you are not yourself but a whole crowd of somebody else. Mary Poppins sighed with pleasure, however, when she saw three of herself, each wearing a blue coat with silver buttons and a blue hat to match. She thought it was such a lovely sight that she wished there had been a dozen of her or even thirty. The more Mary Poppinses the better.

"Come along," she said sternly, as though they had kept *her* waiting. Then they turned the corner and pulled the bell of Number Three, Robertson Road. Jane and Michael could hear it faintly echoing from a long way away and they knew that in one minute, or two at the most, they would be having tea with Mary Poppins's uncle, Mr. Wigg, for the first time ever.

"If he's in, of course," Jane said to Michael in a whisper.

At that moment the door flew open and a thin, watery-looking lady appeared.

"Is he in?" said Michael quickly.

"I'll thank you," said Mary Poppins, giving him a terrible glance, "to let *me* do the talking."

"How do you do, Mrs. Wigg," said Jane politely.

"Mrs. Wigg!" said the thin lady, in a voice even thinner than herself. "How dare you call me Mrs. Wigg? No, thank you! I'm plain Miss Persimmon *and* proud of it. Mrs. Wigg indeed!" She seemed to be quite upset, and they thought Mr. Wigg must be a very odd person if Miss Persimmon was so glad not to be Mrs. Wigg.

"Straight up and first door on the landing," said Miss Persimmon, and she went hurrying away down the passage saying: "Mrs. Wigg indeed!" to herself in a high, thin, outraged voice.

Jane and Michael followed Mary Poppins upstairs. Mary Poppins knocked at the door.

"Come in! Come in! And welcome!" called a loud, cheery voice from inside. Jane's heart was pitter-pattering with excitement.

"He *is* in!" she signaled to Michael with a look.

Mary Poppins opened the door and pushed them in front of her. A large cheerful room lay before them. At one end of it a fire was burning brightly and in the centre stood an enormous table laid for tea—four cups and saucers, piles of bread and butter, crumpets, coconut cakes, and a large plum cake with pink icing.

"Well, this is indeed a Pleasure," a huge voice greeted them, and Jane and Michael looked round for its owner. He was nowhere to be seen. The room appeared to be quite empty. Then they heard Mary Poppins saying crossly: "Oh, Uncle Albert—not *again*? It's not your birthday, is it?"

And as she spoke she looked up at the ceiling. Jane and Michael looked up too and to their surprise saw a round, fat, bald man who was hanging in the air without holding on to anything. Indeed, he appeared to be *sitting* on the air, for his legs were crossed and he had just put down the newspaper which he had been reading when they came in.

"My dear," said Mr. Wigg, smiling down at the children, and looking apologetically at Mary Poppins, "I'm very sorry, but I'm afraid it *is* my birthday."

"Tch, tch, tch!" said Mary Poppins.

"I only remembered last night and there was no time then to send you a postcard asking you to come another day. Very distressing, isn't it?" he said, looking down at Jane and Michael.

"I can see you're rather surprised," said Mr. Wigg. And, indeed, their mouths were so wide open with astonishment that Mr. Wigg, if he had been a little smaller, might almost have fallen into one of them.

"I'd better explain, I think," Mr. Wigg went on calmly. "You see, it's this way. I'm a cheerful sort of man and very disposed to laughter. You wouldn't believe, either of you, the number of things that strike me as being funny. I can laugh at pretty nearly everything, I can."

And with that Mr. Wigg began to bob up and down, shaking with laughter at the thought of his own cheerfulness.

"Uncle Albert!" said Mary Poppins, and Mr. Wigg stopped laughing with a jerk.

"Oh, beg pardon, my dear. Where was I? Oh, yes. Well, the funny thing about me is — all right, Mary, I won't laugh if I can help it! — that whenever my birthday falls on a Friday, well, it's all up with me. Absolutely U.P.," said Mr. Wigg.

"But why — ?" began Jane.

"But how — ?" began Michael.

"Well, you see, if I laugh on that particular day I become so filled with Laughing Gas that I simply can't keep on the ground. Even if I smile it happens. The first funny thought, and I'm up like a balloon. And until I can think of something serious I can't get down again." Mr. Wigg began to chuckle at that, but he caught sight of Mary Poppins's face and stopped the chuckle, and continued: "It's awkward, of course, but not unpleasant. Never happens to either of you, I suppose?"

Jane and Michael shook their heads.

"No, I thought not. It seems to be my own special habit. Once, after I'd been to the Circus the night before, I laughed so much that— would you believe it?— I was up here for a whole twelve hours, and couldn't get down till the last stroke of midnight. Then, of course, I came down with a flop because it was Saturday and not my birthday anymore. It's rather odd, isn't it? Not to say funny?

"And now here it is Friday again and my birthday, and you two and Mary P. to visit me. Oh, Lordy, Lordy, don't make me laugh, I beg of you —" But although Jane and Michael had done nothing very amusing, except to stare at him in astonishment, Mr. Wigg began to laugh again loudly, and as he laughed he went bouncing and bobbing about in the air, with the newspaper rattling in his hand and his spectacles half on and half off his nose.

He looked so comic, floundering in the air like a great human bubble, clutching at the ceiling sometimes and sometimes at the gas-bracket as he passed it, that Jane and Michael, though they were trying hard to be polite, just couldn't help doing what they did. They laughed. *And* they laughed. They shut their mouths tight to prevent the laughter from escaping, but that didn't do any good. And presently they were rolling over and over on the floor, squealing and shrieking with laughter.

"Really!" said Mary Poppins. "Really, *such* behaviour!"

"I can't help it, I can't help it!" shrieked Michael as he rolled into the fender. "It's so terribly funny. Oh, Jane, *isn't* it funny?"

Jane did not reply, for a curious thing was happening to her. As she laughed she felt herself growing lighter and lighter, just as though she were being pumped full of air. It was a curious and delicious feeling and it made her want to laugh all the more. And then suddenly, with a bouncing bound, she felt herself jumping through the air. Michael, to his astonishment, saw her go soaring up through the room. With a little bump her head touched the ceiling and then she went bouncing along it till she reached Mr. Wigg.

"*Well!*" said Mr. Wigg, looking very surprised indeed. "Don't tell me it's *your* birthday, too?" Jane shook her head.

"It's not? Then this Laughing Gas must be catching! Hi — whoa there, look out for the mantelpiece!" This was to Michael, who had suddenly risen from the floor and was swooping through the air, roaring with laughter, and just grazing the china ornaments on the mantelpiece as he passed. He landed with a bounce right on Mr. Wigg's knee.

"How do you do," said Mr. Wigg, heartily shaking Michael by the hand. "I call this really friendly of you — bless my soul, I do! To come up to me since I couldn't come down to you — eh?" And then he and Michael looked at each other and flung back their heads and simply howled with laughter.

"I say," said Mr. Wigg to Jane, as he wiped his eyes. "You'll be thinking I have the worst manners in the world. You're standing and you ought to be sitting — a nice young lady like you. I'm afraid I can't offer you a chair up here, but I think you'll find the air quite comfortable to sit on. I do."

Jane tried it and found she could sit down quite comfortably on the air. She took off her hat and laid it down beside her and it hung there in space without any support at all.

"That's right," said Mr. Wigg. Then he turned and looked down at Mary Poppins.

"Well, Mary, we're fixed. And now I can enquire about *you*, my dear. I must say, I am very glad to welcome you and my two young friends here today—why, Mary, you're frowning. I'm afraid you don't approve of—er—all this."

He waved his hand at Jane and Michael, and said hurriedly: "I apologise, Mary, my dear. But you know how it is with me. Still, I must say I never thought my two young friends here would catch it, really I didn't, Mary! I suppose I should have asked them for another day or tried to think of something sad or something—"

"Well, I must say," said Mary Poppins primly, "that I have never in my life seen such a sight. And at your age, Uncle—"

"Mary Poppins, Mary Poppins, do come up!" interrupted Michael. "Think of something funny and you'll find it's quite easy."

"Ah, now do, Mary!" said Mr. Wigg persuasively.

"We're lonely up here without you!" said Jane, and held out her arms towards Mary Poppins. "*Do* think of something funny!"

"Ah, *she* doesn't need to," said Mr. Wigg, sighing. "She can come up if she wants to, even without laughing—and she knows it." And he looked mysteriously and secretly at Mary Poppins as she stood down there on the hearth-rug.

"Well," said Mary Poppins, "it's all very silly and undignified, but, since you're all up there and don't seem able to get down, I suppose I'd better come up, too."

With that, to the surprise of Jane and Michael, she put her hands down at her sides and without a laugh, without even the faintest glimmer of a smile, she shot up through the air and sat down beside Jane.

"How many times, I should like to know," she said snappily, "have I told you to take off your coat when you come into a hot room?" And she unbuttoned Jane's coat and laid it neatly on the air beside the hat.

"That's right, Mary, that's right," said Mr. Wigg contentedly, as he leant down and put his spectacles on the mantelpiece. "Now we're all comfortable—"

"There's comfort *and* comfort," sniffed Mary Poppins.

"And we can have tea," Mr. Wigg went on, apparently not noticing her remark. And then a startled look came over his face.

"My goodness!" he said. "How dreadful! I've just realised— that table's down there and we're up here. What *are* we going to do? We're here and it's there. It's an awful tragedy— awful! But oh, it's terribly comic!" And he hid his face in his handkerchief and laughed loudly into it. Jane and Michael, though they did not want to miss the crumpets and the cakes, couldn't help laughing, too, because Mr. Wigg's mirth was so infectious.

Mr. Wigg dried his eyes.

"There's only one thing for it," he said. "We must think of something serious. Something sad, very sad. And then we shall be able to get down. Now— one, two, three! Something *very* sad, mind you!"

They thought and thought, with their chins on their hands.

Michael thought of school, and that one day he would have to go there. But even that seemed funny today and he had to laugh.

Jane thought: I shall be grown up in another fourteen years!

But that didn't sound sad at all but quite nice and rather funny. She could not help smiling at the thought of herself grown up, with long skirts and a handbag.

"There was my poor old aunt Emily," thought Mr. Wigg out loud. "She was run over by an omnibus. Sad. Very sad. Unbearably sad. Poor Aunt Emily. But they saved her umbrella. That was funny, wasn't it?" And before he knew where he was, he was heaving and trembling and bursting with laughter at the thought of Aunt Emily's umbrella.

"It's no good," he said, blowing his nose. "I give it up. And my young friends here seem to be no better at sadness than I am. Mary, can't *you* do something? We want our tea."

To this day Jane and Michael cannot be sure of what happened then. All they know for certain is that, as soon as Mr. Wigg had appealed to Mary Poppins, the table below began to wriggle on its legs. Presently it was swaying dangerously, and then with a rattle of china and with cakes lurching off their plates onto the cloth, the table came soaring through the room, gave one graceful turn, and landed beside them so that Mr. Wigg was at its head.

"Good girl!" said Mr. Wigg, smiling proudly upon her. "I knew you'd fix something. Now, will you take the foot of the table and pour out, Mary? And the guests on either side of me. That's the idea," he said, as Michael ran bobbing through the air and sat down on Mr. Wigg's right. Jane was at his left hand. There they were, all together, up in the air and the table between them. Not a single piece of bread-and-butter or a lump of sugar had been left behind.

Mr. Wigg smiled contentedly.

"It is usual, I think, to begin with bread-and-butter," he said to Jane and Michael, "but as it's my birthday we will begin the wrong way—which I always think is the *right* way—with the Cake!"

And he cut a large slice for everybody.

"More tea?" he said to Jane. But before she had time to reply there was a quick, sharp knock at the door.

"Come in!" called Mr. Wigg.

The door opened, and there stood Miss Persimmon with a jug of hot water on a tray.

"I thought, Mr. Wigg," she began, looking searchingly round the room, "you'd be wanting some more hot—well, I never! I simply *never!*" she said, as she caught sight of them all seated on the air round the table. "Such goings-on I never did see. In all my born days I never saw such. I'm sure, Mr. Wigg, I always knew *you* were a bit odd. But I've closed my eyes to it—being as how you paid your rent regular. But such behaviour as this—having tea in the air with your guests—Mr. Wigg, sir, I'm astonished at you! It's that undignified, and for a gentleman of your age—I never did—"

"But perhaps you will, Miss Persimmon!" said Michael.

"Will what?" said Miss Persimmon haughtily.

"Catch the Laughing Gas, as we did," said Michael.

Miss Persimmon flung back her head scornfully.

"I hope, young man," she retorted, "I have more respect for myself than to go bouncing about in the air like a rubber ball on the end of a bat. I'll stay on my own feet, thank you, or my name's not Amy Persimmon, and—oh dear, oh *dear,* my goodness, oh DEAR—what *is* the matter? I can't walk, I'm going, I—oh, help, *HELP!*"

For Miss Persimmon, quite against her will, was off the ground and was stumbling through the air, rolling from side to side like a very thin barrel, balancing the tray in her hand. She was almost weeping with distress as she arrived at the table and put down her jug of hot water.

"Thank you," said Mary Poppins in a calm, very polite voice.

Then Miss Persimmon turned and went wafting down again, murmuring as she went: "So undignified—and me a well-behaved, steady-going woman. I must see a doctor—"

When she touched the floor she ran hurriedly out of the room, wringing her hands, and not giving a single glance backwards.

"So undignified!" they heard her moaning as she shut the door behind her.

"Her name can't be Amy Persimmon, because she *didn't* stay on her own feet!" whispered Jane to Michael.

But Mr. Wigg was looking at Mary Poppins—a curious look, half-amused, half-accusing.

"Mary, Mary, you shouldn't—bless my soul, you shouldn't, Mary. The poor old body will never get over it. But, oh, my Goodness, didn't she look funny waddling through the air—my Gracious Goodness, but didn't she?"

And he and Jane and Michael were off again, rolling about the air, clutching their sides and gasping with laughter at the thought of how funny Miss Persimmon had looked.

"Oh dear!" said Michael. "Don't make me laugh any more. I can't stand it! I shall break!"

"Oh, oh, oh!" cried Jane, as she gasped for breath, with her hand over her heart. "Oh, my Gracious, Glorious, Galumphing Goodness!" roared Mr. Wigg, dabbing his eyes with the tail of his coat because he couldn't find his handkerchief.

"IT IS TIME TO GO HOME." Mary Poppins's voice sounded above the roars of laughter like a trumpet.

And suddenly, with a rush, Jane and Michael and Mr. Wigg came down. They landed on the floor with a huge bump, all together. The thought that they would have to go home was the first sad thought of the afternoon, and the moment it was in their minds the Laughing Gas went out of them.

Jane and Michael sighed as they watched Mary Poppins come slowly down the air, carrying Jane's coat and hat.

Mr. Wigg sighed, too. A great, long, heavy sigh.

"Well, isn't that a pity?" he said soberly. "It's very sad that you've got to go home. I never enjoyed an afternoon so much — did you?"

"Never," said Michael sadly, feeling how dull it was to be down on the earth again with no Laughing Gas inside him.

"Never, never," said Jane, as she stood on tip-toe and kissed Mr. Wigg's withered-apple cheeks. "Never, never, never, never . . . !"

They sat on either side of Mary Poppins going home in the Bus. They were both very quiet, thinking over the lovely afternoon. Presently Michael said sleepily to Mary Poppins: "How often does your uncle get like that?"

"Like what?" said Mary Poppins sharply, as though Michael had deliberately said something to offend her.

"Well — all bouncy and boundy and laughing and going up in the air."

"Up in the air?" Mary Poppins's voice was high and angry. "What do you mean, pray, up in the air?"

Jane tried to explain.

"Michael means — is your uncle often full of Laughing Gas,

71

and does he often go rolling and bobbing about on the ceiling when—"

"Rolling and bobbing! What an idea! Rolling and bobbing on the ceiling! You'll be telling me next he's a balloon!" Mary Poppins gave an offended sniff.

"But he did!" said Michael. "We saw him."

"What, roll and bob? How dare you! I'll have you know that my uncle is a sober, honest, hard-working man, and you'll be kind enough to speak of him respectfully. And don't bite your Bus ticket! Roll and bob, indeed—the idea!"

Michael and Jane looked across Mary Poppins at each other. They said nothing, for they had learnt that it was better not to argue with Mary Poppins, no matter how odd anything seemed.

But the look that passed between them said: "Is it true or isn't it? About Mr. Wigg. Is Mary Poppins right or are we?"

But there was nobody to give them the right answer.

The Bus roared on, wildly lurching and bounding.

Mary Poppins sat between them, offended and silent, and presently, because they were very tired, they crept closer to her and leant up against her sides and fell asleep, still wondering. . . .

Talk

retold by Harold Courlander

*What would you do if every-
thing around you suddenly started
talking? A funny folktale from
West Africa.*

A farmer went out to his field one morning to dig up some yams. While he was digging, one of the yams said to him, "Well, at last you're here. You never weeded me, but now you come around with your digging stick. Go away and leave me alone!"

The farmer turned around and looked at his cow in amazement. The cow was chewing her cud and looking at him.

"Did you say something?" he asked.

The cow kept on chewing and said nothing, but the man's dog spoke up.

"It wasn't the cow who spoke to you," the dog said. "It was the yam. The yam says leave him alone."

The man became angry, because his dog had never talked before, and he didn't like his tone besides. So he took his knife and cut a branch from a palm tree to whip his dog. Just then the palm tree said, "Put that branch down!"

The man was getting very upset about the way things were going, and he started to throw the palm branch away, but the palm branch said, "Man, put me down softly!"

He put the branch down gently on a stone, and the stone said, "Hey, take that thing off me!"

This was enough, and the frightened farmer started to run for his village. On the way he met a fisherman going the other way with a fish trap on his head.

"What's the hurry?" the fisherman asked.

"My yam said, 'Leave me alone!' Then the dog said, 'Listen to what the yam says!' When I went to whip the dog with a palm branch, the tree said, 'Put that branch down!' Then the palm branch said, 'Do it softly!' Then the stone said, 'Take that thing off me!'"

"Is that all?" the man with the fish trap asked. "Is that so frightening?"

"Well," the man's fish trap said, "did he take it off the stone?"

"Wah!" the fisherman shouted. He threw the fish trap on the

ground and began to run with the farmer, and on the trail they met a weaver with a bundle of cloth on his head.

"Where are you going in such a rush?" he asked them.

"My yam said, 'Leave me alone!'" the farmer said. "The dog said, 'Listen to what the yam says!' The tree said, 'Put that branch down!' The branch said, 'Do it softly!' And the stone said, 'Take that thing off me!'"

"And then," the fisherman continued, "the fish trap said, 'Did he take it off?'"

"That's nothing to get excited about," the weaver said, "no reason at all."

"Oh, yes, it is," his bundle of cloth said. "If it happened to you, you'd run, too!"

"Wah!" the weaver shouted. He threw his bundle on the trail and started running with the other men.

They came panting to the ford in the river and found a man bathing.

"Are you chasing a gazelle?" he asked them.

The first man said breathlessly, "My yam talked to me, and it said, 'Leave me alone!' And my dog said, 'Listen to your yam!' And when I cut myself a branch, the tree said, 'Put that branch down!' And the branch said, 'Do it softly!' And the stone said, 'Take that thing off me!'"

The fisherman panted, "And my trap said, 'Did he?'"

The weaver wheezed, "And my bundle of cloth said, 'You'd run, too!'"

"Is that why you're running?" the man in the river asked.

"Well, wouldn't you run if you were in their position?" the river said.

The man jumped out of the water and began to run with the others. They ran down the main street of the village to the house of the chief. The chief's servants brought his stool out, and he came and sat on it to listen to their complaints. The men began to recite their troubles.

"I went out to my garden to dig yams," the farmer said, waving his arms. "Then everything began to talk! My yam said, 'Leave me alone!' My dog said, 'Pay attention to your yam!' The tree said, 'Put that branch down!' The branch said, 'Do it softly!' And the stone said, 'Take it off me!'"

"And my fish trap said, 'Well, did he take it off?'" the fisherman said.

"And my cloth said, 'You'd run, too!'" the weaver said.

"And the river said the same," the bather said hoarsely, his eyes bulging.

The chief listened to them patiently, but he couldn't refrain from scowling.

"Now, this is really a wild story," he said at last. "You'd better all go back to your work before I punish you for disturbing the peace."

76

So the men went away, and the chief shook his head and mumbled to himself, "Nonsense like that upsets the community."

"Fantastic, isn't it?" his stool said. "Imagine, a talking yam!"

The Big Cheese

by Miriam Schlein

A farmer has a present for the king—a beautiful cheese. But no one will believe his claim that it's the best cheese in all the land without first trying a taste. . . .

Once there was a farmer who made a big cheese. It was yellow, and mellow, and round. It was a most beautiful cheese.

"Without a doubt," said the farmer, "this is the best cheese that has ever been made in all the land."

"I think you are right," said his wife. "Take it to the market. It will fetch a good price."

"No," said the farmer. "The best cheese in all the land—who should eat it? Not just anybody! I am going to present this cheese to the king!"

"To the king?" asked his wife.

"Of course," said the farmer.

He placed the big cheese carefully in a wheelbarrow. His wife draped it over with a snowy-white linen napkin. And the farmer went down the road, pushing the cheese before him.

He had not gone far when he met a goatherd, herding a flock of goats.

"What are you pushing along in that barrow, my friend?" called out the goatherd.

"A cheese," replied the farmer. "I am on my way to present it to the king, for it is the finest cheese that has ever been made in the land."

"Indeed?" said the goatherd. "And is it made of goat's milk?"

"No," said the farmer. "Cow's milk."

"Then how," said the goatherd, "can it be the best cheese ever made? The best cheeses are *always* made from goat's milk."

"How?" said the farmer indignantly. "This is how!" He flung the napkin off. And there sat the cheese—that beautiful, yellow, mellow cheese.

"It does look fine," agreed the goatherd. "But have you tasted it?"

"Of course not," said the farmer. "You can see it is still whole."

"Then how do you *know* it is the finest cheese ever made?" said the goatherd. "We must taste it, here and now."

"Stop!" cried the farmer. "How can I present the king with a cheese that has a piece cut out of it?"

"But how can you present the king with a cheese you do not *know* tastes the best?" said the goatherd.

"You are right," said the farmer. "Cut."

They each took a small taste.

"Indeed," sighed the goatherd. "I must admit you have made the finest cheese a man could make, out of goat's milk *or* cow's milk."

The farmer beamed. He threw his napkin over the cheese, and he went on his way.

The road went over hill and dale. It did not seem long before night began to fall.

He came to an inn.

I will stop here, he thought. I will have a bite to eat and get a good night's rest, and early in the morning I shall be on my way.

He pushed open the door and entered a cheerful room, with a crackling fire in the fireplace. A fat, jolly-looking man was seated before it.

"Come in," cried the man. "The innkeeper is in the kitchen, fixing my meal. Come warm yourself by the fire, my friend. I am a traveler like yourself."

The farmer parked the barrow with the cheese carefully away from the heat of the fire.

"What have you there, that you treat with such care?" asked the man.

"This is a cheese, which I am taking to the king," replied the farmer.

"Are you!" cried the man. "What good fortune that I stopped here tonight! For I am a cheese maker, too. I am honored indeed to meet the cheese maker to the king."

"Oh, I am not that," said the farmer modestly. "I am just a farmer. But I have made a cheese so magnificent and fine, I have decided to present it to the king."

"To the king?" said the traveler. "But the king has the most skilled cheese makers in the land, right at the palace!"

"But my cheese is the best that has ever been made in the land," said the farmer.

"The best?" repeated the traveler. "How do you know?"

"I know," said the farmer proudly. "Besides, the goatherd agreed with me."

"The goatherd!" said the traveler. "A goatherd may know about goats—but what does a goatherd know of the king's taste for cheese?

"I tell you what," he went on. "Do me the honor of dining with me. And after we have dined, and our stomachs are contented, then *we*," he said, pointing to himself, "then *we* will taste your cheese. For it does not do to taste cheese when one is very hungry. For then almost anything will taste delicious."

"But I want to present my cheese to the king!" cried the farmer.

"Of course," said the traveler. "Don't fear. We will just take a teeny taste. It won't even be missed."

The farmer sighed and sat down. What a jolly stout man like

this meant by "a teeny taste" he did not exactly know, but he could well imagine!

Presently the innkeeper came and set before them all sorts of steaming hot dishes. Roast duck, all crispy and brown, and mushrooms. And buttery beans, and a tray of fresh baked bread. And to drink, a pitcher of homemade root beer.

"Ah," sighed the farmer when they were finished. "That was a meal to remember."

"And now," said the traveling cheese maker, "we come to the treat. Now we taste the cheese."

"Are you sure you want to taste it now?" asked the farmer. "Aren't you a bit full?"

"Of course I'm full," cried the cheese maker. "But if your cheese is as delicious as you say, we will enjoy it even if we are full as full as full."

He whisked the napkin off the cheese.

"It *looks* good," he said.

He leaned over the cheese.

"It *smells* good," he said.

Then he cut the cheese and took a small wedge. He bit into the soft center, and crushed the cheese on his tongue, and swallowed.

"But the taste!" he cried, striking the table. "The taste is magnificent! I have never tasted as good a cheese — not even one made by myself! May I just take another small piece?"

"Please do," said the farmer, nodding.

"Mmmm," said the fat cheese maker with his mouth full. "You are right. This is a cheese fit for a king. May I take just one more taste?"

"Of course," said the farmer, not knowing what else he could say.

"This is the last," said the fat cheese maker, carving a large slice.

The farmer leaped up, threw his napkin over the cheese, and trundled it away.

Now that the cheese maker had eaten, he seemed little disposed to talk. So the farmer said good night and went up to sleep. In the morning, when he awoke, the other traveler had already gone. So the farmer had breakfast alone. Then he took his wheelbarrow, with the cheese, and trundled it down the road.

The road is straight; the day is fine. I should be there soon, he thought.

Toward noontime he noticed that the road was beginning to change. It no longer led straight along but had turned into a lazy meandering kind of road — as if whoever ventured upon it could never be much in a hurry.

If a great tree stood in the way, the road looped around it. When it reached a little brook, the road took a sharp turn and went alongside.

The farmer stopped to rest and looked around. Can this possibly be the road to the palace? he wondered. This lazy, meandering road? I should think the king's road would be broad and straight, so his men could ride down it ten abreast on horseback. Perhaps I took a wrong turn somewhere.

As he was wondering this, a swineherd came down the road. He was so busy trying to make his pigs move along in an orderly fashion that at first he did not even notice the farmer sitting there.

"Hello there," said the farmer. "Is this the way to the king's palace?"

"The only way," said the swineherd, who was now busy poking and prodding a pink pig with black spots who had decided to lie down and go to sleep.

"Thank you," said the farmer. Imagine, he thought. He is the first person not to ask me what I have in my wheelbarrow. Lucky thing it is, too.

The farmer lifted the handles to his barrow and trundled along. And soon, in the distance, he saw four tall spires, reaching into the sky.

"The king's palace," he said. "I am there at last!" He straightened his shirt and pulled up his socks. It was not long before he presented himself at the palace gate.

"Who are you, and what do you carry?" asked the guard at the gate.

"I am a farmer. And this is a cheese I have made for the king."

"That door," said the guard. He pointed across the courtyard. "There is the royal kitchen."

"But this cheese is to be presented to the king himself!" said the farmer determinedly.

"Oh," said the guard. He pointed to a high, arched doorway.

The farmer trundled across the courtyard and through the high arched doorway. He found himself in a large hall. From behind a closed door at the end of the hall, he heard a hum of voices.

He sat down on the edge of a high white chair.

"Ahem. Ahem." He cleared his throat. He did not know what to do.

But presently the door opened. A man came out. He was dressed in elegant ribbons and silk, with a plumed hat on his head.

"What is that?" he said, looking at the wheelbarrow.

Aye, what a boor I was, to wheel a barrow into the king's own hall, thought the farmer. "A big cheese," he said. "I wish to present it to the king."

"A cheese, you say?" said the man. "Ah, a bit of cheese would taste good. Besides, I am the king's taster. Whatever the king eats, I must taste first. To make sure it is all right, you understand."

He bent down and with his silver penknife cut a wedge of the cheese.

"Indeed," he said with his mouth full. "It is a fine cheese."

Just then, the door opened again. And another man came out. He was even more elegantly dressed than the first.

"What is that?" he asked in amazement, seeing the farmer and his barrow.

"Cheese," said the taster. "Very good."

"Ah," said the second man, unclasping a little gold penknife and making a cut.

The farmer smiled and felt more at ease. If they like my cheese, I am sure the king will, too, he thought.

More of the king's men came out. Soon there were seven, all standing about, munching on the cheese.

The farmer looked on happily, although a bit worried now.

I am glad they all like it, he thought. But what will be left for the king?

Presently still another man came out. He had a ruddy face, as if he spent much of his time out of doors. And he was not dressed as splendidly as the other men of the court.

"What is this?" he said.

"A cheese, sir," said the farmer, stepping forward. "The best that has ever been made. I have come to present it to the king!"

"Indeed?" said the ruddy-faced man, lifting the napkin.

The farmer stared. What was left of his big cheese? Not a half. Not even a quarter. Just a small piece stood there, amidst the crumbles.

The ruddy-faced man bent down and reached for the last piece.

"Stop!" cried the farmer. "Stop, stop, STOP!"

The others looked up in amazement.

"Excuse me," said the farmer sadly. "But I meant this cheese for the king. And you are taking the very last piece. Well, take it," he said sadly. "It doesn't matter now. I can't present the king with just a scrap. Go on. Finish it."

The seven elegant men stepped back. The ruddy-faced man stood alone.

"But I am the king," he said softly.

"The king!" said the farmer. "A thousand pardons!" He fell to one knee, nearly tipping the barrow as he did so.

"Come," said the king. "Get up. A thousand pardons for what? For your loyalty to the king? For wishing to present him with the finest cheese you have ever made in your life? Come now," he said. "Get up."

The farmer got up, all red in the face.

"May I have this last piece of cheese now?" asked the king with a smile. "I do love cheese, you know."

"Of course." The farmer nodded.

The king ate the piece of cheese.

"It is the finest cheese I have ever tasted!" he said. "And I thank you."

The farmer beamed. "But such a small piece was left," he said.

"Look here," said the king. "This is not the last cheese you will ever make, is it?"

"No." The farmer shook his head.

"Well, then," said the king, "when you make another cheese that you feel you would like me to have, just bring it around. And do not let anyone taste it first," he added.

To this the farmer agreed. Then he trundled his empty wheelbarrow back home, whistling all the way.

How glad he was to be home! He told his wife of his adventures. Then he busied himself with his chickens, and his cows, and his asparagus and pumpkin garden. And of course, he made cheeses.

They were fine cheeses, yellow and mellow and round. But somehow, none seemed yellow and mellow enough so as to be fit for a king.

Many months passed. Then one day, the farmer ran in to his wife.

"I have made one!" he cried. "At last!"

"Fit for a king?" asked his wife.

"Fit for a king!"

They placed the big cheese on the wheelbarrow, and the farmer set off once again to the palace of the king.

No one got a taste of *this* cheese.

This cheese the farmer presented to the king, round and complete.

It was every bit as good as the first one. It was a cheese fit for a king!

That is what the king said.

And he should know!

The Wonderful Pearl

by James Riordan

What would you do if you found a pearl that would make any wish come true? Find out what Wa wishes for in this touching folktale from Vietnam.

Once upon a time, there was an orphan girl called Wa, who lived on the banks of the Mekong River. Ever since she had been a little girl and could carry a basketful of rice upon her back, she had worked for the village headman.

Like the other villagers, she toiled long and hard for her master, and was hardly given enough to eat in return. She had to cut down the biggest trees that even the strongest men could barely fell. And when the rice was ripe, she had to peel the husks from dawn till dusk. Her hands were always blistered from cutting wood, and when the skin had hardened, her palms would itch from the coarse rice husks. Each night she would gather herbs to put on her raw, itching hands, and other workers would come to her for their wounds to be soothed—for she had a great knowledge of wild plants and their healing powers.

One day she was cleaning the new harvest of rice with her friend Ho. Ho was so thin that his ribs stuck through his tattered shirt. As they worked, they spoke of the drudgery of their lives and wondered, sadly, how many of their people would die of starvation before the year was out.

Before long, the headman's messenger arrived and ordered Wa to guard the rice house, which stood on piles close by the paddy field. The rice house was filled to the roof with stores of rice, and the hungry girl longed to eat some, but she was ever mindful of the master's warning: "An evil spirit protects my rice. If you eat even one grain, the spirit will jump inside you. Then you will die and turn into a grain of rice!"

In her fear, poor Wa went hungry.

As darkness came, Wa was overcome with tiredness, and she fell asleep. In her dreams she saw her master growing fat and rich from the store of rice, which grew bigger and bigger from the toil of her fellow villagers, while they grew thin and sick.

All of a sudden, she was rudely awakened by a vicious kick in her side. It was the headman's son. "You lazy pig!" he screamed in her ear. "Fill this pail with water by my return."

Wa jumped up in alarm as he went laughing on his way. She took the pail and ran swiftly to the river to fill it up.

The waters of the river were ruffled by a gentle breeze as they lapped softly at the girl's sore and aching feet. She sighed and bent down to fill the pail. All of a sudden, the waters began to foam and ring out like the *torong's* twanging strings, making her scamper back to dry land in fear.

Out of the silver foam appeared a maiden, tall and proud, wearing a long shimmering dress. She approached Wa and, taking her trembling hand, softly said, "The Water Spirit's young

daughter has fallen ill. And our sprites say that you, Wa, are wise with herbs and can cure her. Come with me and see the girl."

"No, no, I cannot," Wa cried out. "I have to guard the rice house. The master would kill me if he should find me gone."

"Do not anger us, Wa. The Water Spirit is mightier even than your village chief. If you do not come, the sprites will punish you."

A dry pathway suddenly opened before her, and the stately maid led Wa down into the underwater depths.

Wa was told that the Water Spirit's daughter had had a scorpion sting while playing on the shore. Ever since she had been ill. All the underwater doctors — the shrimps and eels — were fussing about the poor sick girl, but none could cure the strange sickness that had overcome her. For three months she had lain in a fever, unable to eat or sleep.

Wa gently touched the wound and told the sprites what

herbs they should collect. When these were ready, she used them on the girl, and three days later she was well.

The Water Spirit was overjoyed. "Dear Wa," he said, "what will you take as reward?"

"My only wish is to save my people from need," Wa replied.

Thereupon, the Spirit handed her a precious pearl, saying, "This pearl will make any wish come true."

Wa thanked the Water Spirit and returned to dry land along the underwater path. When she reached the rice house, she saw in horror the tracks of birds, big and small, all around it. They had helped themselves to half the unprotected rice!

An old man passed by just then, and stared at Wa in surprise. "Where did you get to, Wa, these past three months?" he said. "Be warned, for you're in trouble. Just look about you: Those thieving birds have stolen the master's rice. He is searching for you, and his rage is terrible."

Wa went sadly on her way. Eventually she sat down on the ground and hung her head in woe. Her thin dress became drenched with tears. And then, all at once, she remembered the precious pearl. Taking out the Spirit's gift, she murmured, "Pearl, wonderful pearl, bring me rice to eat."

Right away, a huge bamboo dish of rice appeared before her, filled with all manner of tasty food. And at her back a store of rice grew up three times higher than the master's rice house.

She clapped her hands with joy and began to eat to her heart's content. Yet suddenly she stopped. Her thoughts were of her dear friend Ho. He, too, was poor and had to toil in the master's paddy fields all day. So she took out the pearl again and said, "Pearl, wonderful pearl, bring me a house, a pair of oxen and some hens. And then bring my friend Ho to me."

Hardly had Wa spoken than, to her right, a tall house on bamboo stilts grew up, with hens scratching round about; and there beneath it was a pair of milk-white oxen. Inside the house

she saw gongs and copper pans, a brass kettle on a stove and jars of candy. Just then an astonished Ho appeared, and together they walked into the house as Wa told him her wonderful story.

Next morning Wa made her way to the headman's house. As soon as he set eyes on the girl, he roared like a stricken ox.

"Ahrr-rrr, here comes the lump of oxen dung, the one who stole my rice. I'll have her fed to the tigers in the hills!"

"It was not my fault you lost your rice," Wa spoke up boldly.

"No matter — I'll make up what you lost. Just send your son to collect it."

"Lead on," snarled the headman's son. "I'll take it now. And if you fail by a single grain, I'll bring your head back on a tray."

When the son set eyes on Wa's rich house, his mouth dropped open in surprise and his eyes grew wide like a bullock's.

"Hey there, Ho!" shouted Wa. "The master's son has come for rice. Give him all he wants. I'm going to the river to fish."

When the man recovered from his shock, he hurried down to the riverbank and stared at the girl with fresh respect. He thought that she looked stronger and sturdier than the finest jungle tree.

"I do n-n-not want your r-r-rice, dear Wa," he stammered. "I wish to m-m-marry you."

Wa only laughed. "Take your rice and go," she said. "I cannot stand the sight of you."

Slowly he made his way back home and reported all to his father. In a rage, the headman called his guards.

"Gather up your spears, your swords, your bows and arrows," he yelled. "We go to slay that low-born girl and take her riches for ourselves."

But the good people of the village ran swiftly to warn Wa of the master's plans. At once, the bold young girl took out the magic pearl and said, "Pearl, wonderful pearl, protect us from this evil man."

Suddenly a chain of lofty mountains sprang up around the headman's house. He and his men tried to scale the heights. But after three whole months they had managed to climb only an eighth of the mountain, and eventually they had to give up. They were forced to return defeated to their narrow valley and were never able to bother the poor again.

Meanwhile, on the other side of the mountain, Wa and Ho lived in contentment. The wise, just Wa shared out her wealth among the people, who never went hungry again, and she protected them always with her wonderful pearl.

✦ Stories of ✦
You and Me

Two Big Bears

by Laura Ingalls Wilder

Life was very different in the 1860s,
when Laura Ingalls lived with her
pa, ma, and two sisters in a little
house in the wilderness. Read about
one of her adventures in this story
from Little House in the Big
Woods.

One day Pa said that spring was coming.

In the Big Woods the snow was beginning to thaw. Bits of it dropped from the branches of the trees and made little holes in the softening snowbanks below. At noon all the big icicles along the eaves of the little house quivered and sparkled in the sunshine, and drops of water hung trembling at their tips.

Pa said he must go to town to trade the furs of the wild animals he had been trapping all winter. So one evening he made a big bundle of them. There were so many furs that when they were packed tightly and tied together they made a bundle almost as big as Pa.

Very early one morning Pa strapped the bundle of furs on his shoulders, and started to walk to town. There were so many furs to carry that he could not take his gun.

Ma was worried, but Pa said that by starting before sun-up

99

and walking very fast all day he could get home again before dark.

The nearest town was far away. Laura and Mary had never seen a town. They had never seen a store. They had never seen even two houses standing together. But they knew that in a town there were many houses, and a store full of candy and calico and other wonderful things—powder, and shot, and salt, and store sugar.

They knew that Pa would trade his furs to the storekeeper for beautiful things from town, and all day they were expecting the presents he would bring them. When the sun sank low above the treetops and no more drops fell from the tips of the icicles, they began to watch eagerly for Pa.

The sun sank out of sight, the woods grew dark, and he did not come. Ma started supper and set the table, but he did not come. It was time to do the chores, and still he had not come.

Ma said that Laura might come with her while she milked the cow. Laura could carry the lantern.

So Laura put on her coat and Ma buttoned it up. And Laura put her hands into her red mittens that hung by a red yarn string around her neck, while Ma lighted the candle in the lantern.

Laura was proud to be helping Ma with the milking, and she carried the lantern very carefully. Its sides were of tin, with places cut in them for the candlelight to shine through.

When Laura walked behind Ma on the path to the barn, the little bits of candlelight from the lantern leaped all around her on the snow. The night was not yet quite dark. The woods were dark, but there was a gray light on the snowy path, and in the sky there were a few faint stars. The stars did not look as warm and bright as the little lights that came from the lantern.

Laura was surprised to see the dark shape of Sukey, the brown cow, standing at the barnyard gate. Ma was surprised, too.

It was too early in the spring for Sukey to be let out in the Big Woods to eat grass. She lived in the barn. But sometimes on warm days Pa left the door of her stall open so she could come into the barnyard. Now Ma and Laura saw her behind the bars, waiting for them.

Ma went up to the gate, and pushed against it to open it. But it did not open very far, because there was Sukey, standing against it. Ma said, "Sukey, get over!" She reached across the gate and slapped Sukey's shoulder.

Just then one of the dancing little bits of light from the lantern jumped between the bars of the gate, and Laura saw long, shaggy, black fur, and two little, glittering eyes.

Sukey had thin, short, brown fur. Sukey had large, gentle eyes.

Ma said, "Laura, walk back to the house."

So Laura turned around and began to walk toward the house. Ma came behind her. When they had gone partway, Ma snatched her up, lantern and all, and ran. Ma ran with her into the house, and slammed the door.

Then Laura said, "Ma, was it a bear?"

"Yes, Laura," Ma said. "It was a bear."

Laura began to cry. She hung on to Ma and sobbed, "Oh, will he eat Sukey?"

"No," Ma said, hugging her. "Sukey is safe in the barn. Think, Laura—all those big, heavy logs in the barn walls. And the door is heavy and solid, made to keep bears out. No, the bear cannot get in and eat Sukey."

Laura felt better then. "But he could have hurt us, couldn't he?" she asked.

"He didn't hurt us," Ma said. "You were a good girl, Laura, to do exactly as I told you, and to do it quickly, without asking why."

Ma was trembling, and she began to laugh a little. "To think," she said, "I've slapped a bear!"

Then she put supper on the table for Laura and Mary. Pa had not come yet. He didn't come. Laura and Mary were undressed, and they said their prayers and snuggled into the trundle bed.

Ma sat by the lamp, mending one of Pa's shirts. The house seemed cold and still and strange, without Pa.

Laura listened to the wind in the Big Woods. All around the house the wind went crying as though it were lost in the dark and the cold. The wind sounded frightened.

Ma finished mending the shirt. Laura saw her fold it slowly and carefully. She smoothed it with her hand. Then she did a thing she had never done before. She went to the door and pulled the leather latch-string through its hole in the door, so that nobody could get in from outside unless she lifted the latch. She came and took Carrie, all limp and sleeping, out of the big bed.

She saw that Laura and Mary were still awake, and she said to them: "Go to sleep, girls. Everything is all right. Pa will be here in the morning."

Then she went back to her rocking chair and sat there rocking gently and holding Baby Carrie in her arms.

She was sitting up late, waiting for Pa, and Laura and Mary meant to stay awake, too, till he came. But at last they went to sleep.

In the morning Pa was there. He had brought candy for Laura and Mary, and two pieces of pretty calico to make them each a dress. Mary's was a china-blue pattern on a white ground, and Laura's was dark red with little golden-brown dots on it. Ma had calico for a dress, too; it was brown, with a big, feathery white pattern all over it.

They were all happy because Pa had got such good prices for his furs that he could afford to get them such beautiful presents.

The tracks of the big bear were all around the barn, and there were marks of his claws on the walls. But Sukey and the horses were safe inside.

All that day the sun shone, the snow melted, and little streams of water ran from the icicles, which all the time grew thinner. Before the sun set that night, the bear tracks were only shapeless marks in the wet, soft snow.

After supper Pa took Laura and Mary on his knees and said he had a new story to tell them.

The Story of Pa and the Bear in the Way

"When I went to town yesterday with the furs, I found it hard walking in the soft snow. It took me a long time to get to town, and other men with furs had come in earlier to do their trading. The storekeeper was busy, and I had to wait until he could look at my furs.

"Then we had to bargain about the price of each one, and then I had to pick out the things I wanted to take in trade.

"So it was nearly sundown before I could start home.

"I tried to hurry, but the walking was hard and I was tired, so I had not gone far before night came. And I was alone in the Big Woods without my gun.

"There were still six miles to walk, and I came along as fast as I could. The night grew darker and darker, and I wished for my gun, because I knew that some of the bears had come out of their winter dens. I had seen their tracks when I went to town in the morning.

"Bears are hungry and cross at this time of year; you know they have been sleeping in their dens all winter long with nothing to eat, and that makes them thin and angry when they wake up. I did not want to meet one.

"I hurried along as quick as I could in the dark. By and by the stars gave a little light. It was still black as pitch where the woods were thick, but in the open places I could see, dimly. I could see the snowy road ahead a little way, and I could see the dark woods standing all around me. I was glad when I came into an open place where the stars gave me this faint light.

"All the time I was watching, as well as I could, for bears. I was listening for the sounds they make when they go carelessly through the bushes.

"Then I came again into an open place, and there, right in the middle of my road, I saw a big black bear.

"He was standing up on his hind legs, looking at me. I could see his eyes shine. I could see his pig-snout. I could even see one of his claws, in the starlight.

"My scalp prickled, and my hair stood straight up. I stopped in my tracks, and stood still. The bear did not move. There he stood, looking at me.

"I knew it would do no good to try to go around him.

He would follow me into the dark woods, where he could see better than I could. I did not want to fight a winter-starved bear in the dark. Oh, how I wished for my gun!

"I had to pass that bear to get home. I thought that if I could scare him, he might get out of the road and let me go by. So I took a deep breath, and suddenly I shouted with all my might and ran at him, waving my arms.

"He didn't move.

"I did not run very far toward him, I tell you! I stopped and looked at him, and he stood looking at me. Then I shouted again. There he stood. I kept on shouting and waving my arms, but he did not budge.

"Well, it would do me no good to run away. There were other bears in the woods. I might meet one any time. I might as well deal with this one as with another. Besides, I was coming home to Ma and you girls. I would never get here if I ran away from everything in the woods that scared me.

"So at last I looked around, and I got a good big club, a solid, heavy branch that had been broken from a tree by the weight of snow in the winter.

"I lifted it up in my hands, and I ran straight at that bear. I swung my club as hard as I could and brought it down, *bang!* on his head.

"And there he still stood, for he was nothing but a big, black, burned stump!

"I had passed it on my way to town that morning. It wasn't a bear at all. I only thought it was a bear, because I had been thinking all the time about bears and being afraid I'd meet one."

"It really wasn't a bear at all?" Mary asked.

"No, Mary, it wasn't a bear at all. There I had been yelling, and dancing, and waving my arms, all by myself in the Big Woods, trying to scare a stump!"

Laura said, "Ours was really a bear. But we were not scared, because we thought it was Sukey."

Pa did not say anything, but he hugged her tighter.

"Oo-oo! That bear might have eaten Ma and me all up!" Laura said, snuggling closer to him. "But Ma walked right up to him and slapped him, and he didn't do anything at all. Why didn't he do anything?"

"I guess he was too surprised to do anything, Laura," Pa said. "I guess he was afraid, when the lantern shone in his eyes. And when Ma walked up to him and slapped him, he knew *she* wasn't afraid."

"Well, you were brave, too," Laura said. "Even if it was only a stump, you thought it was a bear. You'd have hit him on the head with a club, if he *had* been a bear, wouldn't you, Pa?"

"Yes," said Pa, "I would. You see, I had to."

Then Ma said it was bedtime. She helped Laura and Mary undress and button up their red flannel nightgowns. They knelt down by the trundle bed and said their prayers.

"Now I lay me down to sleep,
I pray the Lord my soul to keep.
If I should die before I wake,
I pray the Lord my soul to take."

Ma kissed them both, and tucked the covers in around them. They lay there awhile, looking at Ma's smooth, parted hair and her hands busy with sewing in the lamplight. Her needle made little clicking sounds against her thimble, and then the thread went softly, *swish!* through the pretty calico that Pa had traded furs for.

Laura looked at Pa, who was greasing his boots. His mustache and his hair and his long brown beard were silky in the lamplight, and the colors of his plaid jacket were gay. He whistled cheerfully while he worked, and then he sang:

"The birds were singing in the morning,
And the myrtle and the ivy were in bloom,
And the sun o'er the hills was a-dawning,
'Twas then that I laid her in the tomb."

It was a warm night. The fire had gone to coals on the hearth, and Pa did not build it up. All around the little house in the Big Woods, there were little sounds of falling snow, and from the eaves there was the drip, drip of the melting icicles.

In just a little while the trees would be putting out their baby leaves, all rosy and yellow and pale green, and there would be wildflowers and birds in the woods.

Then there would be no more stories by the fire at night, but all day long Laura and Mary would run and play among the trees, for it would be spring.

The Report Card

by Johanna Hurwitz

*When first grader Russell gets a bad
mark on his report card, he decides
that he's not the only one in his
family who "needs improvement."
A laugh-out-loud story from the
popular* Russell Sprouts.

One of the things that made first grade different from
kindergarten was that in first grade the teacher sent a report
card home to your parents. Russell had heard about report
cards from Nora and Teddy. He had been very proud when he
had gotten his report card for the first time in the fall. In the
winter Russell had received his card with new marks on it. And
now that it was spring, Mrs. Evans gave out the cards once
again.

"Your parents will be eager to see your progress," she told
the class. "Don't forget. After your parents read them, they
should sign their names on the bottom line. Then return the
cards to me, please."

Russell studied his yellow card. It was like a little folder, and
there were words written on all four sides. The first time he had

seen his card, he could only read his name on it. But now he had become such a good reader that he was able to read almost all the words on the card. He was not surprised that Mrs. Evans had marked "Excellent" next to the boxes for Reading Readiness Skills and Manual Dexterity and Arithmetic Skills. Russell knew that he was one of the best readers in the class. Already he had completed two workbooks and he had begun a third one. Some of the boys and girls in his class were still using the first workbook that Mrs. Evans had given them in September when they entered the class.

Once again Mrs. Evans reminded everyone that the boxes said "Excellent," "Good," "Fair," and "Needs Improvement." "I have checked the boxes that best describe each of you," she said.

Russell turned his card over. He saw that something was written on the back and the box was marked "Needs Improvement."

"What's back here?" Russell called out.

"On the back of the card, it tells about your class behavior," Mrs. Evans explained. "Calling out without raising your hand is not good behavior."

Russell often called out. He couldn't help it. If he waited until Mrs. Evans noticed that his hand was in the air, it took too long. Sometimes Russell just had to shout out.

When Russell went home from school that day he put his report card in his lunch box as Mrs. Evans had suggested. That way his mother would find the card and it wouldn't get lost.

Mrs. Michaels read her son's card. "Your father and I are proud of you. You are doing very good work," she told him. "I can hardly believe how much you have learned. And I'm sure your behavior will be getting better soon, too. Don't you think so?"

"Maybe," said Russell. He was a little angry that Mrs. Evans hadn't marked the "Good" box about that.

"I want another cookie," he said, finishing the two that his mother had given him, along with some milk, as an after-school snack.

"No more cookies now," said Mrs. Michaels. "You don't want to spoil your appetite for supper."

"Yes, I do," complained Russell. But Mrs. Michaels didn't give him any more.

After supper, Russell wanted to watch television. But his father wanted to watch a special news broadcast at the same time. Russell didn't care about news. It was too boring to watch men and women talking about things that he didn't understand.

"It's not fair that you get to watch what you want and I don't," said Russell.

"This is an important program," said Mr. Michaels. "Why don't you go play in your room so that I can see it in peace."

"I wish we had two television sets," he complained to his father.

"I wish you would keep quiet so that I can hear this program," Mr. Michaels responded.

"This is my home," said Russell angrily. "I can talk if I want to."

"You can go and talk in your bedroom!" shouted his father. "Go there right now. And stay there!"

Russell stormed out of the living room. He didn't care if he couldn't stay and watch television or talk to his father. He didn't want to talk to his father anyhow. His father was so mean to him.

Russell sat down on his bed to decide what he should do. From his room he could hear his mother giving Elisa her bath. His mother didn't care that he couldn't watch TV or talk with his father in the living room. Russell felt angry with his mother, too.

Then Russell got an idea. He would make a report card for his parents. He knew just which boxes he would mark. Russell went to his shelf and found a package of colored paper and a black marking pen.

Russell folded a sheet of yellow paper to make it look like his report card. Then he realized that he did not know how to spell important words like *Behavior*. So, even though his father had ordered him to stay in his bedroom, Russell decided to tip-toe into the kitchen to get his report card. He could copy all the words he needed from it.

Elisa was talking in the bathtub as he walked past the open bathroom door. Russell decided she probably thought KiKi was in the bathtub, too. Mrs. Michaels didn't notice Russell and neither did Mr. Michaels, who was watching the television. In the kitchen Russell opened his lunch box, which was still on the counter, removed his report card, and tiptoed back into his room.

Then he began copying from the card:

REPORT CARD
NAME: MOMMY AND DADDY

Even though he was angry at his parents tonight, Russell knew he had to mark the best box for Reading Readiness. They were both good readers and read lots of stories to him. Then he remembered that they weren't always *ready* to read a story whenever he wanted them to. Sometimes his mother said she had to finish cooking supper. Sometimes his father said he was too tired.

So Russell made a box and put a check inside. Underneath the box he wrote, "Reading Readiness — Needs Improvement."

Russell looked at his report card. He didn't think it was so important to give his parents marks for Arithmetic Skills and Manual Dexterity. He decided to use his own words. He wanted to give his parents marks in important things like:

| TV | Needs Improvement |
| Cookys | Needs Improvement |

Presnts	Needs Improvement
Bed Time	Needs Improvement
Yellng	Needs Improvement

Russell covered all four sides of the yellow paper. He drew a line at the bottom so that his parents could sign their names, just like they had to do on his card. He listened hard and could hear the water going down the drain from the bathtub. He knew his mother and Elisa would be coming into the bedroom in another minute. Russell hurried into the kitchen. He put his own report card and the special one that he had made for his parents inside his lunch box. Wouldn't his mother be surprised when she opened it to put in his lunch for tomorrow?

The next morning, when Russell was having breakfast, his father said to him, "Russell, your mother and I received the report card that you made for us."

Russell looked up from his scrambled eggs. He had forgotten about the card in the night while he was sleeping.

"Did you see your marks?" Russell asked.

"Yes," said Mr. Michaels. "I'm sorry to say that we didn't get as good marks as you did."

"You should try harder," said Russell. This morning he did not feel angry at his father. He was a pretty good father, Russell thought. He wouldn't want to have a different one.

"I will try harder at home," said Russell's father, "if you will try harder at school."

"I try very hard at school," said Russell. "But sometimes I forget. I can't help it if I call out to Mrs. Evans."

"I know," said Mr. Michaels. "And I can't help it if I get impatient with you sometimes."

"Too many cookies would make you sick," said Mrs. Michaels to her son.

"A hundred cookies would make me sick," Russell agreed. "But three cookies wouldn't be too much for me. My stomach is much bigger now that I'm in first grade."

"All right," agreed his mother. "You try very hard to raise your hand in class and not to call out. And I'll have three cookies waiting for you when you come home today."

"Good," said Russell. It sounded like a fine plan.

"I've packed your lunch, and your father and I both signed your report card. You have to return it to Mrs. Evans today," said Mrs. Michaels.

"And we've signed the other card, too. Do you want it back?" asked Russell's father.

"You can keep it," said Russell. "I can make another card if you need more improvement."

He put on his jacket to get ready for school. He grinned at his parents. "Mostly you're pretty good," he said.

"Mostly you're pretty good, too," said Mr. Michaels, giving Russell a big hug before he went to work.

A Fruit and Vegetable Man

by Roni Schotter

Sun Ho loves to watch Ruby Rubenstein at work in his fruit and vegetable store. But when Ruby gets sick, there's no one to run the store. Can Sun Ho think of a way to help his friend?

Ruby Rubenstein was a fruit and vegetable man. His motto was "I take care." Six mornings a week, long before the sun was up, Ruby was.

"Is it time, Ruby?" his wife, Trudy, always asked from deep under the covers.

"It's time," Ruby always answered. Then he'd jump out of bed, touch his knees, then his toes, and hurry uptown to market to choose the ripest fruit and vegetables for his store.

For nearly fifty years it had been so — ever since he and Trudy first sailed across the ocean to make a new life together.

Every morning before school, Sun Ho and his sister, Young Mee, who, with their family, had just flown across the sky to make a new life together, came to watch Ruby work his magic.

"Yo-ho, Mr. Ruby!" Sun Ho would call out. "Show me!"

And nodding to Sun Ho, Ruby would pile apples, tangerines, and pears in perfect pyramids, arrange grapes in diamonds, insert a head of lettuce as accent, then tuck in a bunch of broccoli or a bit of watercress for trim.

It was like seeing a great artist at work. Sun Ho felt honored to be there. "Like a painting, Mr. Ruby!" he would say shyly.

Ruby always smiled, and his smile filled Sun Ho with happiness and, deep inside, a strange feeling that was like wishing. Sun Ho watched as Ruby juggled cantaloupes, then cut them into wedges and packed them neatly in plastic. Inside Sun Ho, the feeling that was like wishing grew stronger.

"He's an artist, all right," Old Ella from up the block always said, pocketing an apple and a handful of prunes.

Ruby didn't mind. He'd just wink and utter one wonderful

word: "Taste!" Then he'd offer whatever he had on special that day to Sun Ho, his sister, and anyone who wanted.

"What would we *do* without Ruby?" Mary Morrissey asked the crowd one gray afternoon. The people of Delano Street sighed and shook their heads at such a terrible thought.

"Mr. Ruby," Sun Ho said, "he's one of a kind."

Yes, everyone on Delano Street appreciated Ruby. But Ruby was getting old. Lately, when he got up to touch his knees and his toes, there was a stiffness Ruby pretended he didn't feel and a creaking Trudy pretended she didn't hear. And sometimes, though Ruby never would admit it, there was a wish that he could stay a little longer in bed with Trudy.

"Ruby," Trudy said to him one morning from under the covers. "Long ago you and I made a promise. We said if ever we got old, we'd sell the business and go to live in the mountains. *Is it time, Ruby?*"

"NO!!" Ruby thundered. And he leapt out of bed, did *twice* his usual number of exercises, and ran off to market.

As if to prove he was as young as ever, he worked especially hard at the store that day and made some of his most beautiful designs.

That afternoon, Sun Ho came by as Ruby was arranging potatoes in his own special way. Sun Ho watched as Ruby whirled them in the air and tossed them with such skill that they landed perfectly, one next to the other in a neat row.

"Yo-ho, Mr. Ruby!" Sun Ho said, filled with admiration. "Teach me?"

Proudly, Ruby grabbed an Idaho and two russets and taught Sun Ho how to juggle. Next he taught him how to pile grapefruits to keep them from falling. By the time Sun Ho's parents stopped by, Ruby had even taught Sun Ho how to work the

register. Then he sat Sun Ho down and told him how, early every morning, he went to market to choose his fruit and vegetables.

"Take me!" Sun Ho pleaded, the feeling that was like wishing so big now he felt he might burst. "Please?"

Ruby thought for only a moment. Then he spoke. "My pleasure," he announced.

So early the next day, while Venus still sparkled in the dark morning sky, Ruby took Sun Ho to market. Sun Ho had an excellent nose, and together he and Ruby sniffed out the most fragrant fruit and sampled the choicest chicory. Then Ruby showed Sun Ho how he talked and teased and argued his way to the best prices.

All the rest of that long day, Sun Ho felt special. And Ruby? He felt, well . . . tired. Whenever Trudy was busy with a customer, Ruby leaned over and pretended to tie his shoe, but what he did, really, was *yawn*. By afternoon, Ruby was running out of the store every few minutes. "The fruit!" he'd yell to Trudy. "Got to fix the fruit!" he'd say, but once outside, what he did, really, was *sneeze*.

"To your health, Mr. Ruby," Sun Ho whispered, sneaking him a handkerchief.

"Thank you, Mr. Sun Ho," Ruby said, quietly blowing his nose.

That evening it began to snow on Delano Street. It snowed all night, and by morning the street was cold and white, the color of fresh cauliflower.

For the first time in many years, Ruby woke up feeling sick. His face was red, his forehead hot. "No work today," Trudy said. "Ruby's Fruit and Vegetable is closed until further notice." What would the people of Delano Street do without him? Ruby wondered. But he was too sick to care.

When Sun Ho arrived at the store that day and saw that it was closed, he was worried. Where was Ruby?

Upstairs in his bed, Ruby dozed, dreaming of spring and fresh apricots. Once, when he opened his eyes, Sun Ho was standing next to him . . . or was he?

"No worries," Sun Ho seemed to say. "I take care." Then as strangely as he had appeared, Sun Ho disappeared. Was Ruby dreaming?

For the next three days, for the first time in his life, Ruby was too sick to think or worry about his store. He stayed deep under the covers, enjoying Trudy's loving care, and more than that, her barley soup. On the morning of the fourth day, he felt well enough to worry. On the morning of the fifth day, a Saturday, there was no stopping him. "My store!" he shouted. Leaning on Trudy's arms, he put on his clothes. Then he rushed off to reopen.

What a surprise when he arrived! The store was open. In fact, it looked as if it had never been shut. The peppers were in pyramids, the dates in diamonds, the winter tomatoes in triangles. Sun Ho's father was helping Old Ella to a pound of carrots. Sun Ho's mother was at the register. Young Mee was polishing pears. And, in the center of it all, Sun Ho stood smiling, offering customers a taste of something new — bean sprouts!

When they saw Ruby, everyone cheered. Ruby bowed with pleasure.

"I took care, Mr. Ruby!" Sun Ho called out proudly.

"I see," Ruby answered. "You're a fruit and vegetable man, Sun Ho, like me."

Sun Ho's face turned the color of Ruby's radishes. The feeling that was like wishing was gone now. In its place was a different feeling: pride.

"*Is it time,* Ruby?" Trudy whispered.

Ruby sighed. He thought about how much he liked Sun Ho and his family and how carefully they had kept his store. He thought about the stiffness and creaking in his knees. He thought about the mountains and about Trudy's loving care. More than that, he thought about her barley soup.

"It's time," he said finally.

Now Sun Ho is a fruit and vegetable man! Every morning, long before the sun is up, long before it's time for school, Sun Ho and his family are up, ready to hurry to market to choose the ripest fruit and vegetables for their store.

And Ruby? He's still a fruit and vegetable man . . . only now he and Trudy grow their own.

Herbert's Treasure

by Alice Low

Herbert loves collecting. His mother thinks his "treasures" are nothing but junk, but Herbert knows that they might come in handy . . . someday.

Herbert was a treasure collector. He liked everything about collecting treasures.

He liked getting up in the morning and thinking about what he would find that day. He liked leaving his house and going to the old town dump. He liked searching in the big pile of junk near the collapsed old barn, finding treasures, bringing them home, and arranging them in his room.

He liked looking at them, too. Everywhere he looked in his room there was some kind of treasure — hinges, hammer, a mirror, some wire, pieces of glass, and a bicycle tire. He just liked having treasures.

His mother didn't like it, though. It was very hard to clean his room. Every week, day after day, she said, "Herbert, please, Herbert, throw something away!"

"I can't," Herbert said. "They're treasures."

"Junk!" said his mother. "Nothing but junk!"

"You never know," Herbert said. "They might come in handy — someday."

"This rusty can?" his mother said.

"I can keep things in it," Herbert said. He picked up three screws, four nails, and a doorbell and put them in the can.

When his mother left, he dumped them out to look at them. The doorbell didn't work, but it might — someday. Most of all, he liked thinking about his treasures and what he could do with them — someday.

And so every afternoon — in rain or sun — when other boys were playing baseball or going to the movies, Herbert went to the abandoned dump. By himself, so he wouldn't have to share his treasures. He found a rusty saw, a clock with no hands, a

screwdriver, bricks, and some paint pots and pans and carried them home.

His mother said, "Why do you go to that messy dump when our yard is so neat and nice and we have croquet and a swing and everything just right for *you?*"

"It's more fun in the dump," Herbert said.

"Get rid of that junk, Herbert, right now, today. Herbert, please, Herbert, throw *something* away!"

"Okay," Herbert said. "Tomorrow."

The next day he brought back a broken shovel, some chair rungs from chairs, bedposts and table legs, stair treads from stairs. And a real find—a lock. He put them on top of his toys on the shelves.

"Now look at your toys!" his mother said. "All squashed under that junk. I *mean* it, Herbert, right now, today. *Please, Herbert, please,* throw something away."

"All right," Herbert said. He took everything off his shelves and made two piles—one to keep and one to throw away.

Then he threw away the throwaway pile. After he'd arranged his treasures on his toy shelves, he thought about the lock. It didn't work, but it might—someday.

Every day he brought home more—windowpanes, picture frames, planks from old floors, shingles and doorknobs and frames from old doors. The mountain in the dump got smaller and smaller. . . .

And his room got more and more crowded. He had to make a path through the treasures to get to his bed. And it was very hard to open the door.

It was exciting to look around his room, but it was sad to go to the dump now because there was almost nothing left to find. The only treasure left was an old carved door.

He dragged it home on his wagon—slowly. He needed time to figure out where to put it. By the time he got to his room he knew.

But first he had to sweep out the treasures from under his bed. There was only one place to put *them*—on top of his bed. Finally, he slid the door under his bed. That night he slept on the floor.

The next morning his mother was furious. She said, "This is the limit. I mean it. Today! Herbert, please, Herbert, throw something away!"

"Don't worry, there's nothing more to find," said Herbert sadly. "Unless—maybe—there's something *under*ground."

And he set out with his shovel and began to dig. Digging was harder, but more fun, too, because you never knew what might be under there.

Mostly there were rocks. Then one day his shovel struck something hard that went *clang!* Metal! Only metal rang that way.

He dug it up, scratched off the dirt, and washed it with the hose until he could see what it was. A key!

It didn't fit the car door, or the kitchen door, or the front door. But it had to open something somewhere. Nobody would make a key that didn't open anything.

He polished it, put it under his pillow, and thought about it every night. It might be the key to a chest full of gold pieces. Then he could buy anything he wanted. He'd like that. Except where would he put all the new things?

Maybe it was the key to a castle dungeon. He would rescue the princess imprisoned there. Then he'd be a hero.

Or maybe—this was even better—a key to the *whole* castle, where he'd be the king. Not a castle full of gold thrones and red carpets; an empty castle with nothing in it—except his treasures. And nobody else would live there. It would be his own castle, where no one could say, "Herbert, please, Herbert, throw something away!"

He could see it in his dream. And he could see himself coming in the door with more and more treasures. The door was old and carved and nobody else could open it because *he* had the key. He could see the lock, too, rusty and old.

He woke up. The moon was shining on the rusty lock. He took the key from under his pillow, and slowly, his heart thumping, tried the key in the lock. It didn't fit. Maybe it was upside down. He turned it around. It still didn't fit. Not quite. He oiled the lock and tried the key again. This time it fit! He turned it slowly. *CLICK!* the lock opened. The key fit the lock!

And the lock fit the door! He screwed it in and screwed on the doorknob — and then he went to sleep.

In the morning he woke up and saw the door with the key in the lock. And he remembered. It was going to be a busy day. He had a plan.

First he dragged everything outdoors. His mother didn't ask what he was doing. She was just glad he was doing it — outdoors.

He sawed and hammered for three days until he was almost finished. Then he set in the doorframe and hinged on the door. And finally, he opened the door with his key and moved everything in.

Then he hammered some more, and painted some, too. There were plenty of shelves — shelves for his paint pots and clock with no hands, his tire and his wire and his tools and his pans. And for everything else.

Last of all, he moved himself in. It *was* a castle, just like the one in his dream. The floorboards were warped, and the windows were cracked, but there was plenty of room — room for his treasures and no one to say, "Herbert, please, Herbert, throw something away!"

The doorbell still doesn't work, but it might — someday.

The Cat That Could Fly

by Joan Tarcher Durden

Cats can't fly. . . .
Or can they?

I have a cat. A soft and fluffy cat, the color of the smoke that swirls out of the smoke hole when my mother is cooking. A pretty, gray Navajo cat named Suce.

Suce has two homes. She lives in my mother's hogan in Chinle, and in my grandmother's hogan a mile away. No one knows when Suce is leaving either of her homes. One moment she's there, and the next she's gone. No one carries Suce from one place to the other. No one sees her walking along the trail.

One morning when I crawl out from under my blanket, there is no one to greet me. My mother is not sitting at the fire cooking. My father is not eating across from the fire. Big Sister is not combing her long hair with the hair broom. And Little Boy is not practicing with the bow and arrow that Grandfather gave him.

I yawn and stretch and look all around the hogan. I look from the dirt floor that Big Sister sweeps every day, to the rounded wall that my father built of juniper and earth, to the fire where my mother left some fried bread for me. My stomach rumbles, so I eat my breakfast.

I pour some goat's milk from the pail into a shallow tin pan and call Suce. But she doesn't come. I call and call. But still Suce doesn't come running for her food. Maybe she is outside hunting for field mice and can't hear me.

I stand at the doorway of my mother's hogan. I look out at the yellow sand and the mountains. I look out at my mother's empty sheep corral, and at my father's horses grazing in the distance. But nowhere do I see Suce.

Mother sits at her rug loom under the brush shelter. "Have you seen Suce?" I ask. Mother shakes her head. She is busy weaving designs into her rug and watching Big Sister and Little Boy herding the sheep.

Father stands at the corral. He is saddling his horse to go to the trading post. "Have you seen Suce?" I ask. But Father shakes his head, too. He is busy fastening the cinch strap around the horse's belly.

"I think I will walk to Grandmother's hogan," I say. "She won't know Suce left here without her breakfast." But Mother says the snakes are out and I'm too little to go alone.

I start to cry. My father comes and stands beside me. He sings a funny song to make me laugh. He tells me I can sit behind him on the horse and he will take me to Grandmother's hogan.

We see no sign of Suce along the winding trail. It is a clear path, not marked by the sharp pointed feet of the sheep, but still we cannot spot her fresh paw prints. All I can see are the hoofprints of Father's horse, showing the way we have come.

When we get to Grandmother's hogan, there is Suce. She is eating breakfast out of a tin plate. Grandfather sits on a wooden box petting her.

"Grandfather, did you see Suce coming?" I ask.

Grandfather shakes his head. He says he has been sitting and looking at the land since sunrise, but he did not see Suce coming up the trail. He says he just raised his arm to scratch his head, and when he put his arm down, Suce was there.

"How did Suce come on the trail unseen?" I ask.

Grandfather looks up at the sky, thinking. "Maybe she flies," he says.

A few days later Suce comes back to my mother's hogan. I have to know if Suce can fly. So I take Big Sister's green hair ribbon and Little Boy's red headband and my yellow kerchief. I tie them all together and I tie them to Suce's tail. I am sure if she flies back to the Grandmother's hogan, someone will see that colorful tail streaking across the sky. Then I will know for sure that Suce can fly.

I can hardly wait for Suce to leave my mother's hogan. But this time she stays and stays. And all that time with the funny green, red, and yellow tail tied to her own tail. As annoying as that false tail must be, she never tries to lose it.

Today Suce finally left my mother's hogan.

And today my uncle is visiting. Uncle says I am silly to think a cat can fly. He offers to take me along the trail and prove to me that Suce walked to Grandmother's hogan.

Uncle saddles his horse. He mounts and pulls me up behind him. It is then that we see my yellow kerchief on the roof of the hogan, and Little Boy's red headband on the highest pole of the sheep corral.

"The wind blew them there," Uncle says.

I am not convinced.

When we get to Grandmother's hogan, we see Big Sister's green hair ribbon on the roof.

"The wind blew it here, too," Uncle says.

I am still not convinced.

Grandfather comes out of the hogan. He is carrying Suce in his arms. "I found this silly cat on the roof," he says to us. "She was all tangled up in a green ribbon, and meowing."

"Grandfather, did Suce fly here?" I ask.

Grandfather looks at Uncle. "Did you see any paw prints on the trail?" he asks.

Uncle watches Suce slide to the ground and run back into the hogan. He says to Grandfather, "We didn't look closely enough. There have to be paw prints along that trail. Everyone knows cats don't fly."

I look up at Grandfather. He gives a little shrug and smiles, so I shrug and smile, too. I know that all cats don't fly. But maybe Suce does.

Rodeo Time

by Mildred Pitts Walter

What does it take to be a
real cowboy? Justin finds out
in this rodeo adventure from
Justin and the Best Biscuits
in the World.

Justin walked through the crowds at the fairgrounds with Grandpa, his chest swelling with happiness. Now he would see the cowboys he had heard so much about in action.

Grandpa guided him through the surging crowd. A tall cowboy hat and high-heeled boots made his slim grandpa look even taller. With a feeling of pride, Justin hitched up his jeans, glad he had brought his cowboy belt with the silver buckle. He wished he had a cowboy hat.

The smells of barbecue, baked beans, and popcorn tempted the crowd. Grandpa ordered barbecued ribs for Justin and a hot link sandwich for himself while Justin ordered tall cold drinks for them both.

All over the arena colorful banners splashed: BILL PICKETT COWBOY RODEO SHOW. Justin whispered, "Grandpa, is there another Bill Pickett?"

Grandpa smiled. "Oh, no. Cowboys today, knowing what a good showman William Pickett was, name their show after him."

Cowboy music got the crowd in a mood for action. First cowboys on lively horses galloped around the arena. Then two clowns ran in. One was a lady dressed in a long skirt and pantalettes. Suddenly a voice over a speaker said, "Howdy, partners. Welcome! The famous Bill Pickett Rodeo is about to get under way. Cowboys and cowgirls will ride, rope, and bulldog. You ready, partners?"

The crowd roared, "Ready!"

Suddenly a bull shot out of a gate like a silver bullet, a cowboy on his back. At first Justin was so scared he couldn't look. The crowed roared its satisfaction. Justin finally peeked through his fingers. The cowboy was still riding. The bull was bucking, pitching, rocking, and rolling. The rider still stayed on, squeezing, hugging, and holding that bull with his legs. Then the bull moved like it was waltzing, and the rider fell to the ground.

Instantly the bull turned and plunged at the rider. Justin screamed, "Watch out!" The clowns rushed in, waving banners of cloth to distract the bull. The bull ran away into the corral.

The next event was the lady clown riding a bull. She seemed hardly able to hang on. The bull tossed her about. Her hat and wig came off. Then her dress came off and Justin knew that it was no lady at all. Everybody laughed.

"Ladies and gentlemen," the voice over the speaker called. "Give the rider a hand. That's Rooster. He's not a clown, but one of our best pickup men. Let's hear it for Rooster, partners."

"What are pickup men, Grandpa?" Justin asked.

"They're men who rescue fallen cowboys or pick them off horses so they won't get trampled.

The cheering was interrupted. "Now, partners, we have the best broncobuster since Jessie Stahl, who rode Glasseye. Watch this cowboy from Laredo, Texas," the announcer said. "He will ride a bronco that's as hot as cayenne pepper and as explosive as a volcano."

"Think he'll be as good as Jessie Stahl, Grandpa?" Justin asked.

Before his grandpa answered, the rider came out on a bucking horse between Rooster and another pickup man. The horse streaked into the arena jumping, spinning, and shaking. With its head down it bucked high in the air. The rider stayed on. The horse pitched, plunged, jumped high, twisting in midair. Still the rider stayed without holding on to the saddle horn.

"Why doesn't he hold on to the saddle, Grandpa?" Justin asked.

"If he touches the saddle horn, he will be disqualified and cannot win a prize."

The crowd, up on its feet, roared while that horse tried to toss the rider. The horse started to run, and the pickup men rushed in and pulled the rider off its back. The rider had won.

The horse ran all over the arena snorting and kicking as the crowd still stood, roaring.

Justin wondered what would happen if that horse jumped over into the stands.

"That rider is good," Grandpa said. "He's young, too. He might outbest Jessie one day, but he isn't there yet."

Then the cowgirls' turn came. Women in pretty costumes rode fast-moving horses around barrels. The crowd watched to see which rider could race around four barrels then back to the field in the shortest time. Justin's heart seemed to stand still as one rider, moving as fast as the wind, rode very close to the barrels. He felt sure she would run into a barrel and fall off her horse. But she didn't touch a single barrel and became the winner. Justin shouted with joy.

When the crowd settled, the announcer was telling about calf roping and of another famous black cowboy, Nate Love. Justin remembered Nate Love, nicknamed Deadwood Dick. He looked at Grandpa and smiled as the announcer went on, "Not only did Nate rope and tie calves; he roped and tied wild mustangs, too. Today, let's watch a young cowboy from Prairie View, Texas, rope and tie calves."

Justin jumped to his feet as a black calf came out of one gate and a cowboy on a horse came out of another. The race was on. Finally the cowboy threw his lasso and stopped the calf. The cowboy slid off his horse, threw the calf to the ground, folded its legs, and tied three of them together. Then he raised his hands to let the judges know he was done. The horse moved slowly backward, tightening the rope just enough to keep the calf in place.

Would the calf stay tied six seconds so the cowboy could win? Justin waited. The calf did not wriggle loose. Justin roared with the crowd. "What will his prize be?" Justin asked.

"Money," Grandpa answered.

At last the event Justin had been waiting for arrived. The bulldogging began. A big black steer with long sharp horns raced out of a gate. Two cowboys on horses shot out after it. Suddenly one of the cowboys jumped off his horse and grabbed the steer's horns. He wrestled the steer to the ground, twisting its head back until its nose was up. This was done so quickly and easily that Justin stood and cheered with the crowd.

"That's the way Bill Pickett did it, eh, Grandpa?"

"Yes, but even faster and easier," Grandpa said.

When Justin was sadly thinking all the fun was over, the voice boomed over the loudspeaker. "All boys and girls ten years and younger can now become cowboys and cowgirls. We are going to let loose some baby Brahman bulls. Three of them will have red ribbons on their tails. The boy or girl who gets a ribbon will win a prize."

Justin listened and wondered if he should try. A cowboy needs a hat, he thought. If only I had a cowboy hat. Suddenly he said to himself, If I win prize money, I will buy a hat. "Grandpa," he asked, "can I try?"

"Sure you can. And bring back a ribbon, you hear?"

Justin waited at the gate with the other boys and girls who also wanted to try. The sharp horsey smell floated over him. He felt good and at ease with the smell he loved so much.

The gate to let the baby Brahmans out opened at the same time as the gate to let the boys and girls onto the field. The scramble was on as the blue-gray Brahmans raced about.

Justin waited. Then he saw a baby bull that he could head off and chase in the opposite direction.

The bull calf stopped and faced Justin. Justin stopped, too. He put his hands on his hips and looked at the bull. Suddenly Justin had an idea. He would grab that bull and wrestle it to the ground and draw cheers from the crowd the way the other cowboys had done.

Justin moved forward. Oh no, he thought. This bull has no horns! A dogie needs horns. As he looked the bull in the eye, it turned and ran away, waving its tail.

A red ribbon fluttered. In the nick of time, Justin snatched it. A winner!

When the judge awarded the prizes, he placed a cowboy hat on Justin's head. The crowd roared. Justin waved the red ribbon and though he knew he could not be heard over the cheers, he shouted anyway. "I'm a real cowboy now, Grandpa!"

Henry and Ribs

by Beverly Cleary

Nothing too exciting has ever happened to Henry—until the day he finds Ribsy. Now if he could just get his new dog home. . . . From the classic book Henry Huggins.

Henry Huggins was in the third grade. His hair looked like a scrubbing brush and most of his grown-up front teeth were in. He lived with his mother and father in a square white house on Klickitat Street. Except for having his tonsils out when he was six and breaking his arm falling out of a cherry tree when he was seven, nothing much happened to Henry.

I wish something exciting would happen, Henry often thought.

But nothing very interesting ever happened to Henry, at least not until one Wednesday afternoon in March. Every Wednesday after school Henry rode downtown on the bus to go swimming at the YMCA. After he swam for an hour, he got on the bus again and rode home just in time for dinner. It was fun but not really exciting.

When Henry left the YMCA on this particular Wednesday, he stopped to watch a man tear down a circus poster. Then, with three nickels and one dime in his pocket, he went to the corner drugstore to buy a chocolate ice cream cone. He thought he would eat the ice cream cone, get on the bus, drop his dime in the slot, and ride home.

That is not what happened.

He bought the ice cream cone and paid for it with one of his nickels. On his ways out of the drugstore he stopped to look at funny books. It was a free look, because he had only two nickels left.

He stood there licking his chocolate ice cream cone and reading one of the funny books when he heard a thump, thump, thump. Henry turned, and there behind him was a dog. The dog was scratching himself. He wasn't any special kind of dog. He was too small to be a big dog but, on the other hand, he was much too big to be a little dog. He wasn't a white dog, because parts of him were brown and other parts were black and in between there were yellowish patches. His ears stood up and his tail was long and thin.

The dog was hungry. When Henry licked, he licked. When Henry swallowed, he swallowed.

"Hello, you old dog," Henry said. "You can't have my ice cream cone."

Swish, swish, swish went the tail. "Just one bite," the dog's brown eyes seemed to say.

"Go away," ordered Henry. He wasn't very firm about it. He patted the dog's head.

The tail wagged harder. Henry took one last lick. "Oh, all right," he said. "If you're that hungry, you might as well have it."

The ice cream cone disappeared in one gulp.

"Now go away," Henry told the dog. "I have to catch a bus for home."

He started for the door. The dog started, too.

"Go away, you skinny old dog." Henry didn't say it very loudly. "Go on home."

The dog sat down at Henry's feet. Henry looked at the dog and the dog looked at Henry.

"I don't think you've got a home. You're awful thin. Your ribs show right through your skin."

Thump, thump, thump replied the tail.

"And you haven't got a collar," said Henry.

He began to think. If only he could keep the dog! He had always wanted a dog of his very own and now he had found a dog that wanted him. He couldn't go home and leave a hungry dog on the street corner. If only he knew what his mother and father would say! He fingered the two nickels in his pocket. That was it! He would use one of the nickels to phone his mother.

"Come on, Ribsy. Come on, Ribs, old boy. I'm going to call you Ribsy because you're so thin."

The dog trotted after the boy to the telephone booth in the corner of the drugstore. Henry shoved him into the booth and shut the door. He had never used a pay telephone before. He had to put the telephone book on the floor and stand on tiptoe on it to reach the mouthpiece. He gave the operator his number and dropped his nickel into the coin box.

"Hello — Mom?"

"Why, Henry!" His mother sounded surprised. "Where are you?"

"At the drugstore near the Y."

Ribs began to scratch. Thump, thump, thump. Inside the telephone booth the thumps sounded loud and hollow.

"For goodness' sake, Henry, what's that noise?" his mother demanded. Ribs began to whimper and then to howl. "Henry," Mrs. Huggins shouted, "are you all right?"

"Yes, I'm all right," Henry shouted back. He never could understand why his mother always thought something had happened to him when nothing ever did. "That's just Ribsy."

"Ribsy?" His mother was exasperated. "Henry, will you please tell me what is going on?"

"I'm trying to," said Henry.  Ribsy howled louder. People were gathering around the phone booth to see what was going on. "Mother, I've found a dog. I sure wish I could keep him. He's a good dog and I'd feed him and wash him and everything. Please, Mom."

"I don't know, dear," his mother said. "You'll have to ask your father."

"Mom!" Henry wailed. "That's what you always say!" Henry was tired of standing on tiptoe and the phone booth was getting warm. "Mom, please say

144

yes and I'll never ask for another thing as long as I live!"

"Well, all right, Henry. I guess there isn't any reason why you shouldn't have a dog. But you'll have to bring him home on the bus. Your father has the car today and I can't come after you. Can you manage?"

"Sure! Easy."

"And Henry, please don't be late. It looks as if it might rain."

"All right, Mom." Thump, thump, thump.

"Henry, what's that thumping noise?"

"It's my dog, Ribsy. He's scratching a flea."

"Oh, Henry," Mrs. Huggins moaned. "Couldn't you have found a dog without fleas?"

Henry thought that was a good time to hang up. "Come on, Ribs," he said. "We're going home on the bus."

When the big green bus stopped in front of the drugstore, Henry picked up his dog. Ribsy was heavier than he expected. He had a hard time getting him into the bus and was wondering how he would get a dime out of his pocket when the driver said, "Say, sonny, you can't take that dog on the bus."

"Why not?" asked Henry.

"It's a company rule, sonny. No dogs on buses."

"Golly, Mister, how'm I going to get him home? I just have to get him home."

"Sorry, sonny. I didn't make the rule. No animal can ride on a bus unless it's inside a box."

"Well, thanks anyway," said Henry doubtfully, and lifted Ribsy off the bus.

"Well, I guess we'll have to get a box. I'll get you onto the next bus somehow," promised Henry.

He went back into the drugstore followed closely by Ribsy.

145

"Have you got a big box I could have, please?" he asked the man at the toothpaste counter. "I need one big enough for my dog."

The clerk leaned over the counter to look at Ribsy. "A cardboard box?" he asked.

"Yes, please," said Henry, wishing the man would hurry. He didn't want to be late getting home.

The clerk pulled a box out from under the counter. "This hair tonic carton is the only one I have. I guess it's big enough, but why anyone would want to put a dog in a cardboard box I can't understand."

The box was about two feet square and six inches deep. On one end was printed, DON'T LET THEM CALL YOU BALDY, and on the other, TRY OUR LARGE ECONOMY SIZE.

Henry thanked the clerk, carried the box out to the bus stop, and put it on the sidewalk. Ribsy padded after him. "Get in, fellow," Henry commanded. Ribsy understood. He stepped into the box and sat down just as the bus came around the corner. Henry had to kneel to pick up the box. It was not a very strong box and he had to put his arms under it. He staggered as he lifted it, feeling like the strong man who lifted weights at the circus. Ribsy lovingly licked his face with his wet pink tongue.

"Hey, cut that out!" Henry ordered. "You better be good if you're going to ride on the bus with me."

The bus stopped at the curb. When it was Henry's turn to get on, he had trouble finding the step because he couldn't see his feet. He had to try several times before he hit it. Then he discovered he had forgotten to take his dime out of his pocket. He was afraid to put the box down for fear Ribsy might escape.

He turned sideways to the driver and asked politely, "Will

you please take the dime out of my pocket for me? My hands are full."

The driver pushed his cap back on his head and exclaimed, "Full! I should say they *are* full! And just where do you think you're going with that animal?"

"Home," said Henry in a small voice. The passengers were staring and most of them were smiling. The box was getting heavier every minute.

"Not on this bus, you're not!" said the driver. "But the man on the last bus said I could take the dog on the bus in a box," protested Henry, who was afraid he couldn't hold the dog much longer. "He said it was a company rule."

"He meant a big box tied shut. A box with holes punched in it for the dog to breathe through."

Henry was horrified to hear Ribsy growl. "Shut up," he ordered.

Ribsy began to scratch his left ear with his left hind foot. The box began to tear. Ribsy jumped out of the box and off the bus and Henry jumped after him. The bus pulled away with a puff of exhaust.

"Now see what you've done! You've spoiled everything." The dog hung his head and tucked his tail between his legs. "If I can't get you home, how can I keep you?"

Henry sat down on the curb to think. It was so late and the clouds were so dark that he didn't want to waste time looking for a big box. His mother was probably beginning to worry about him.

People were stopping on the corner to wait for the next bus. Among them Henry noticed an elderly lady carrying a large paper shopping bag full of apples. The shopping bag gave him an idea. Jumping up, he snapped his fingers at Ribs and ran back into the drugstore.

"You back again?" asked the toothpaste clerk. "What do you want this time? String and paper to wrap your dog in?"

"No, sir," said Henry. "I want one of those big nickel shopping bags." He laid his last nickel on the counter.

"Well, I'll be darned," said the clerk, and handed the bag across the counter.

Henry opened the bag and set it up on the floor. He picked up Ribsy and shoved him hind feet first into the bag. Then he pushed his front feet in. A lot of Ribsy was left over.

The clerk was leaning over the counter watching. "I guess I'll have to have some string and paper, too," Henry said, "if I can have some free."

"Well! Now I've seen everything." The clerk shook his head as he handed a piece of string and a big sheet of paper across the counter.

Ribsy whimpered, but he held still while Henry wrapped the paper loosely around his head and shoulders and tied it with the string. The dog made a lumpy package, but by taking one handle of the bag in each hand Henry was able to carry it to the bus stop. He didn't think the bus driver would notice him. It was getting dark and a crowd of people, most of them with packages, was waiting on the corner. A few spatters of rain hit the pavement.

This time Henry remembered his dime. Both hands were full, so he held the dime in his teeth and stood behind the woman with the bag of apples. Ribsy wiggled and whined, even though Henry tried to pet him through the paper. When the bus stopped, he climbed on behind the lady, quickly set the bag down, dropped his dime in the slot, picked up the bag, and squirmed through the crowd to a seat beside a fat man near the back of the bus.

"Whew!" Henry sighed with relief. The driver was the same one he had met on the first bus! But Ribs was on the bus at last. Now if he could only keep him quiet for fifteen minutes they would be home and Ribsy would be his for keeps.

The next time the bus stopped Henry saw Scooter McCarthy, a fifth grader at school, get on and make his way through the crowd to the back of the bus.

Just my luck, thought Henry. I'll bet he wants to know what's in my bag.

"Hi," said Scooter.

"Hi," said Henry.

"Whatcha got in that bag?" asked Scooter.

"None of your beeswax," answered Henry.

Scooter looked at Henry. Henry looked at Scooter. Crackle, crackle, crackle went the bag. Henry tried to hold it more tightly between his knees.

"There's something alive in that bag!" Scooter said accusingly.

"Shut up, Scooter!" whispered Henry.

"Aw, shut up yourself!" said Scooter. "You've got something alive in that bag!"

By this time the passengers at the back of the bus were staring at Henry and his package. Crackle, crackle, crackle. Henry tried to pat Ribsy again through the paper. The bag crackled even louder. Then it began it wiggle.

"Come on, tell us what's in the bag," coaxed the fat man.

"N-n-n-nothing," stammered Henry. "Just something I found."

"Maybe it's a rabbit," suggested one passenger. "I think it's kicking."

"No, it's too big for a rabbit," said another.

"I'll bet it's a baby," said Scooter. "I'll bet you kidnapped a baby!"

"I did not!"

Ribs began to whimper and then to howl. Crackle, crackle, crackle. Thump, thump, thump. Ribsy scratched his way out of the bag.

"Well, I'll be doggoned!" exclaimed the fat man, and began to laugh. "I'll be doggoned!"

"It's just a skinny old dog," said Scooter.

"He is not! He's a good dog."

Henry tried to keep Ribsy between his knees. The bus lurched around a corner and started to go uphill. Henry was thrown against the fat man. The frightened dog wiggled away from him, squirmed between the passengers, and started for the front of the bus.

"Here, Ribsy, old boy! Come back here," called Henry, and started after him.

"Eeek! A dog!" squealed the lady with the bag of apples. "Go away, doggie, go away!"

Ribsy was scared. He tried to run and crashed into the lady's bag of apples. The bag tipped over and the apples began to roll toward the back of the bus, which was grinding up a steep hill. The apples rolled around the feet of the people who were

standing. Passengers began to slip and slide. They dropped their packages and grabbed one another.

Crash! A high-school girl dropped an armload of books.

Rattle! Bang! Crash! A lady dropped a big paper bag. The bag broke open and pots and pans rolled out.

Thud! A man dropped a coil of garden hose. The hose unrolled and the passengers found it wound around their legs.

People were sitting on the floor. They were sitting on books and apples. They were even sitting on other people's laps. Some of them had their hats over their faces and their feet in the air.

Skree-e-etch! The driver threw on the brakes and turned around in his seat just as Henry made his way through the apples and books and pans and hose to catch Ribsy.

The driver pushed his cap back on his head.

OK, sonny," he said to Henry. "Now you know why dogs aren't allowed on buses!"

"Yes, sir," said Henry in a small voice. "I'm sorry."

"You're sorry! A lot of good that does. Loot at this bus! Look at those people!"

"I didn't mean to make any trouble," said Henry. "My mother said I could keep the dog if I could bring him home on the bus."

The fat man began to snicker. Then he chuckled. Then he laughed and then he roared. He laughed until tears streamed down his cheeks and all the other passengers were laughing, too, even the man with the hose and the lady with the apples.

The driver didn't laugh. "Take that dog and get off the bus!" he ordered. Ribsy whimpered and tucked his tail between his legs.

The fat man stopped laughing. "See here, driver," he said, "you can't put that boy and his dog off in the rain."

"Well, he can't stay on the bus," snapped the driver.

Henry didn't know what he was going to do. He guessed he'd have to walk the rest of the way home. He wasn't sure he knew the way in the dark.

Just then a siren screamed. It grew louder and louder until it stopped right alongside the bus.

A policeman appeared in the entrance. "Is there a boy called Henry Huggins on this bus?" he asked.

"Oh, boy, you're going to be arrested for having a dog on the bus!" gloated Scooter. "I'll bet you have to go to jail!"

"I'm him," said Henry in a very small voice.

"I am he," corrected the lady with the apples, who had been a schoolteacher and couldn't help correcting boys.

"You'd better come along with us," said the policeman.

"Boy, you're sure going to get it!" said Scooter.

"Surely going to get it," corrected the apple lady.

Henry and Ribsy followed the policeman off the bus and into the squad car, where Henry and the dog sat in the backseat.

"Are you going to arrest me?" Henry asked timidly.

"Well, I don't know. Do you think you ought to be arrested?"

"No, sir," said Henry politely. He thought the policeman was joking, but he wasn't sure. It was hard to tell about grown-ups sometimes. "I didn't mean to do anything. I just had to get Ribsy home. My mother said I could keep him if I could bring him home on the bus."

"What do you think?" the officer asked his partner, who was driving the squad car.

"We-e-ell, I think we might let him off this time," answered the driver. "His mother must be pretty worried about him if she called the police, and I don't think she'd want him to go to jail."

"Yes, he's late for his dinner already. Let's see how fast we can get him home."

The driver pushed a button and the siren began to shriek. Ribsy raised his head and howled. The tires sucked at the wet pavement and the windshield wipers splip-splopped. Henry began to enjoy himself. Wouldn't this be something to tell the kids at school! Automobiles pulled over to the curb as the police car went faster and faster. Even the bus Henry had been on had to pull over and stop. Henry waved to the passengers. They waved back. Up the hill the police car sped and around the corner until they came to Klickitat Street and then to Henry's block and then pulled up in front of his house.

Henry's mother and father were standing on the porch waiting for him. The neighbors were looking out of their windows.

"Well!" said his father after the policeman had gone. "It's about time you came home. So this is Ribsy! I've heard about you, fellow, and there's a big bone and a can of Feeley's Flea Flakes waiting for you."

"Henry, what *will* you do next?" sighed his mother.

"Golly, Mom, I didn't do anything. I just brought my dog home on the bus like you said."

Ribsy sat down and began to scratch.

The Magic Shell and Making New Friends

by Nicholasa Mohr

Jaime Ramos wishes more than anything that his family had stayed in the beautiful Dominican Republic instead of moving to New York. Will Jaime be able to make a place for himself in this new land?

Another week passed in New York City, and things were as boring as ever for Jaime. His dad was busy working every day and didn't have time to take Jaime out with him. His mom was busy fixing up their large apartment and taking care of little Marietta, who had caught another cold.

Jaime found himself stuck indoors and without friends. He was becoming more and more restless and unhappy. One morning at breakfast, he complained to his dad.

"I have no one to play with. I don't understand this language. I want to go back home!"

"This is your home now and you'd better get used to living here," commanded his dad. "So that's that! We don't want to hear you whine anymore."

"In a few weeks your records should be here from the Dominican Republic. Then you're going to school," his mother reminded Jaime. "You'll learn English and meet other children and make friends."

"And in the meantime, I'll teach you to say a few words," said his father, who was the only one in the family who could speak English.

Jaime nodded sadly; after all, what else could he do?

"Jaime, look on the bright side," said his mom. "Even though we're not having a big Christmas this year, you'll be having a birthday at the beginning of March. We'll have a party for you. You might get those skates or that sled you wanted. I know you'll like that."

Jaime knew she was trying to cheer him up but it didn't work. It only reminded him of how lonely he was.

"How can I go skating or sledding and have a party without any friends?" protested Jaime. They had been in New York City for almost three weeks and he had not made a single friend. "I hate it here! I hate it! I do, I do!" he shouted, then ran to his room and slammed his door.

His parents looked at each other helplessly. It seemed there was no way to make their son happy.

"Why am I in this terrible place, trapped indoors?" sighed Jaime as he sat miserably on his bed.

He thought about his wonderful village, where he was free to run and play. He wondered what Wilfredo, Lucy, and Sarita were doing right now, at this very moment.

Just then he spotted the box that Tío Ernesto had given him. It sat on top of his desk. How did it get there? he wondered. Jaime had put the box away when they arrived and never gave it another thought. He hadn't even seen it since they'd moved in. Now here it was!

Jaime opened the box and took out the conch shell. He

turned it over and examined it carefully. It didn't look very special to Jaime. In fact, it looked quite ordinary.

But as Jaime held the shell, Tío Ernesto's words came back to him . . . as if his great-uncle were right in his room speaking:

All of your memories are stored inside this shell. When you become homesick for Montaña Verde, this special shell will comfort you. You must be quiet and concentrate and listen carefully. You will hear the roaring sea and soon you will have memories of home — of our mountain village, where the skies touch heaven and the earth smiles down at the sea.

Jaime held the shell up to his ear, just as Tío Ernesto had shown him. At first he heard nothing. But soon he began to hear the splashing waves — then the roaring sea. The shell fluttered gently in his hands. Then it began to sparkle. Soon its glow got brighter and brighter until a rainbow appeared.

Streaks of golden light swept across the ceiling and floor.

He felt the carpet vibrate, and blades of grass sprouted up from under his slippers. Trees appeared, and Jaime felt the warm sunshine and smelled the sweetness of honeysuckle and jasmine. Birds chirped and bees gathered pollen from the flowers. . . .

"Hey, Jaime, let's play tag!" Wilfredo tapped Jaime's shoulder and shouted, "Tocao, you're it!" Lucy and Sarita called out to him. Jaime raced to the top of the hill and tagged Sarita, who tagged Wilfredo. They ran and laughed and chased each other along the path up to Tío Ernesto's cabin. Tío Ernesto invited them inside for some cool, sweet lemonade, made with lemons from his lemon tree.

Jaime swung in the hammock while his friends sat on wooden stools. Tío Ernesto had often told them stories about his worldly travels. His cabin was filled with lots of artifacts from his journeys around the world. Today, he held up a large ceremonial mask. "This is from the west coast of Africa. Many of our ancestors were brought here from West Africa by the Spaniards as captive slaves." Then Jaime picked up his favorite wooden carving. Every time he visited his great-uncle's cabin, he always played with the statue of the little boy sitting on a rock fishing in the river.

"I made that carving myself, right here," Tío Ernesto told them.

Jaime really loved that carving. It always made him feel good just to hold it.

"Jaime . . . Jaime! What are you doing, son?" He heard his mother's voice.

When Jaime blinked, there was his mother standing beside him. Once again everything in his room was just as before.

"What are you doing playing with that conch shell?" she asked.

Jaime saw that his shell had become ordinary again.

"Tío Ernesto gave it to me as a going-away present."

"What a strange gift! What are you going to do with it?" she asked.

"I'm going to keep it for good luck," he said, and put his shell safely away.

Every day after that, Jaime went into his room and closed the door. He would listen to the roaring sea and wait for the shell to take him back to Montaña Verde. There he played *la gallinita ciega,* blindman's buff. He played *escondido,* hide-and-go-seek. He followed his friends to the shallow riverbed to catch tadpoles. He ate delicious homemade *dulce de leche,* milk candy. Jaime was home once more, and he was very happy.

Soon his parents began to worry. "You spend too much time in your room," they kept telling him. But Jaime wouldn't listen to them. He was busy having great adventures with his best buddies in the warm sunshine of Montaña Verde.

Making New Friends

When Jaime woke up on Christmas morning, he was excited. He ran into the living room expecting to find lots of presents just as he had every Christmas back home. But all he saw were two stockings, one for him and one for Marietta. More than anything, Jaime had wished for his sled or the ice skates, or some other great surprise. But instead, he got a new truck, some clothes, and a new schoolbag with pencils, a sharpener, and an eraser. It was hard to hide his disappointment.

"It's for when you go to your new school," his mother said.

"Stop sulking," his father scolded. "You don't know how lucky you are—living in this fine apartment and having toys to spare. There are kids who go hungry and have nothing and never even own a toy. So, cut it out!"

Jaime was tired of his father always telling him how lucky he was. He didn't have one friend, and he didn't feel lucky at all. If it weren't for his shell, Jaime would really have been miserable.

One morning just as he finished another wonderful visit to Montaña Verde and was putting away his shell, he heard loud voices from the kitchen.

"All he does is stay in his room. We must do something with that boy!" shouted his father. "Jaime's got to get out of this apartment and into the fresh air."

His mother agreed, and they decided that from now on, she would take him out for a walk every day. Jaime wasn't happy about that and still griped about all the clothes he had to wear. "I can't move and I don't want to play by myself."

"Never mind," insisted his mom. "The cold makes your cheeks rosy. Besides, I must go shopping and take Marietta for her walk and you cannot stay alone."

Jaime shrugged; he knew he had to go whether he liked it or not.

On their way back from shopping that afternoon, Jaime spotted some kids running and having fun in the playground inside their apartment complex.

"Let's go into the playground," said his mom, hoping to get Jaime interested in playing outdoors. "I'd like to put Marietta on the swings."

"Okay," said Jaime. His mom was pleased he agreed, and found an empty bench on the sunny side of the playground.

Jaime spotted the kid with red hair who had smiled at him

in the elevator. The kid stopped bouncing his ball when he seemed to notice Jaime, too. He slowly edged his way over, and the two boys smiled at each other.

The boy continued bouncing his ball as if he were waiting for Jaime to say something. But Jaime suddenly became shy. What could I say to him? he thought. After all, I can't speak English.

Jaime watched, disappointed, as the boy ran off to play with the other boys.

"I think that boy wants to play with you," said his mother.

"But, what can I do about it?" he asked.

"You could say hello. Your father has taught you a few words of English. Why don't you try it out?" urged his mom.

But Jaime had not been very cooperative whenever his dad attempted to teach him English. Now he was sorry he hadn't paid attention.

Just then the ball rolled over to the bench where he was sitting with his mom. Jaime grabbed it and threw it back.

"Thanks!" yelled the boy, and waved at Jaime, who waved back.

"There," said his mom, "why don't you go over and play?"

"No, I don't want to," answered Jaime. "What if they don't like me?"

"I know that boy likes you," she said.

But Jaime was feeling too shy about going over to the kids he didn't know, and insisted on going home.

At dinner that evening, he spoke to his dad.

"Dad, help me again with my English."

"That's my boy!" said his dad, who was very pleased that Jaime was finally taking an interest in learning English. After they finished dinner, his dad taught him to say, "Hello, my name is Jaime," and "How are you? I'm fine," and "Good-bye."

The next afternoon, his mother took Jaime back to the playground, but when he saw that none of the kids were there, he was disappointed. He pushed Marietta on the swings and waited. After a while he took her back to the bench where his mom sat.

"Might as well go home," he told his mom. Just as they were about to leave, he saw the friendly redheaded boy arrive with the other children. This time he waved to Jaime, and a few minutes later he came over.

Bouncing his ball a few times, the boy smiled at Jaime. "Hi! I'm Peter. Who are you?"

Jaime understood. He pointed to himself and tried to answer just as his dad had taught him.

"Hello. *Me llamo Jaime.* Jaime!"

Peter turned to his friends and explained that Jaime didn't speak English. They all nodded and smiled at Jaime.

"You want to play, Jaime?" asked Peter, and pointed to Jaime, then himself, and then signaled toward the other kids.

"Go on, Jaime," coaxed his mom. "Go on. He wants you to play."

"Come on," said Peter, and motioned with his hand for Jaime to come along with him.

"Go on and play," his mom urged Jaime. "We'll be right here if you want to come back. Marietta is happy in her stroller."

Jaime rushed off with Peter. They went to the monkey bars. Peter pointed to each kid and called out their names.

"This is Kevin and Gina and Sheila. His name is Jaime."

Jaime was so excited that he couldn't remember any of their names.

"Let's play follow the leader," said Kevin. "Follow me!" yelled Peter.

Jaime didn't understand what they said, but he followed the others and copied whatever they did. He climbed the monkey bars, went on the seesaw, took giant steps. It was so much fun.

"What school do you go to?" Kevin asked Jaime.

Jaime shrugged. He understood that Kevin was asking something about his school. But he did not know how to answer.

"Jaime can't speak English too good," said Peter. "I heard his mom talking to him in Spanish. I think he only speaks Spanish."

Jaime smiled. "Spanish, *si, si,*" he said, nodding. Then the kids said something else and everyone laughed. Jaime laughed, too, although he didn't know what was said. All he knew was that he hadn't had this much fun since he'd moved to New York.

All too soon, Jaime heard his mother calling. It was already time to go home. He wanted to play some more and asked his mother if they could stay a little longer. But she told him it was time to go home so she could start making supper.

"Come out and play again, Jaime," said Peter. "See you!" yelled the kids.

"See you," echoed Jaime. Then he remembered his lessons with his dad and added, "Good-bye. I'm fine!" The children laughed and laughed.

Jaime smiled and waved. They made him so happy.

That night, when Jaime went to bed, he could hardly wait to see his friends again the next day.

On the very next afternoon as his mom was getting Marietta ready to go out to the playground, Jaime looked out of his window. Something was different. Snowflakes filled the air! They fell, swirling and dancing before his eyes! The city was being covered in a blanket of snow.

It never snowed in Montaña Verde. It was a tropical climate and too hot for snow. Even on Christmas you could play in the warm sunshine and go swimming.

Jaime had seen snow in books and pictures, but he'd never seen the real thing. Back home, everyone had only talked about snow. There was a popular folktale, told to the kids by the storytellers of the Spanish Caribbean. It was about how snow came to be. Many kids believed it to be true. "Snow is magic," the story went, "because when the Sun God is asleep, the angels in heaven get very cold and they cry. Their tears freeze into flakes. As the flakes fall to earth, they turn into snow.

"When the Sun God wakes up, the snow melts. The angels become warm again and smile. Until next time."

Some of the kids believed snow was really magic and so had Jaime. But his dad had told him that snow was not magic.

He explained that snow was formed from the vapor of frozen water high up in the atmosphere.

Jaime had listened but he had not understood all of what his dad had told him. He still wondered if the story about the angels really could be true. Sometimes Jaime would stare at the clouds, searching to see if he could find any angels.

"Is snow really magic?" he whispered. Now he would see for himself!

Jaime rushed to find his mother and little sister and hurry them along. "Snow! Mami . . . snow!" Marietta laughed and pointed outside. The city was covered in white.

His mom dressed Marietta and made sure Jaime had on his muffler and boots. Then they all went outdoors and headed over to the playground.

Jaime felt his heart beating. How would the snowflakes feel? How would they taste?

He removed a glove and felt the gentle flakes melt instantly in his hand.

They looked like the drops of morning mist that fell over Montaña Verde during sunrise. Jaime licked his palm and tasted cold fresh water just like in the riverbed back home.

When he got to the playground, Jaime heard the kids calling out his name. They waved and he waved back as he slid and slipped over to them.

All afternoon they chased each other and tumbled onto a cushion of powdery snow. They tried to make snow people, but the snow was too soft. Jaime, Peter, and Kevin even had a soft snowball fight against Sheila and Gina.

"Isn't this fun?" yelled Peter.

"Isn't this fun?" mimicked Jaime.

"You're a funny kid!" said Sheila, and Jaime laughed along with all the other kids.

This was just as great as playing back home with his buddies. What was even better was that all of the kids lived in the same apartment complex. That meant they could meet in the playground and play together every day.

Later that night, just before he fell asleep, Jaime thought about his shell. But when he went to find the box, it was nowhere to be seen. Jaime yawned; he was too tired to search for the shell.

"I'm also too tired to visit Montaña Verde right now," yawned Jaime, and he dozed off into a deep sleep.

That night he dreamed about riding a shiny red sled in the snow and racing along on a pair of super ice skates with all of his new friends.

The Velveteen Rabbit
or How Toys Become Real

by Margery Williams

The classic story of a young boy's love for his toy rabbit, and how that love makes his rabbit real.

There was once a velveteen rabbit, and in the beginning he was really splendid. He was fat and bunchy, as a rabbit should be; his coat was spotted brown and white, he had real thread whiskers, and his ears were lined with pink sateen. On Christmas morning, when he sat wedged in the top of the Boy's stocking, with a sprig of holly between his paws, the effect was charming.

There were other things in the stocking, nuts and oranges and a toy engine, and chocolate almonds and a clockwork mouse, but the Rabbit was quite the best of all. For at least two hours the Boy loved him, and then Aunts and Uncles came to dinner, and there was a great rustling of tissue paper and unwrapping of parcels, and in the excitement of looking at all the new presents the Velveteen Rabbit was forgotten.

For a long time he lived in the toy cupboard or on the nursery floor, and no one thought very much about him. He was naturally shy, and being only made of velveteen, some of the more expensive toys quite snubbed him. The mechanical toys were very superior, and looked down upon everyone else; they were full of modern ideas, and pretended they were real. The model boat, who had lived through two seasons and lost most of his paint, caught the tone from them and never missed an opportunity of referring to his rigging in technical terms. The Rabbit could not claim to be a model of anything, for he didn't know that real rabbits existed; he thought they were all stuffed with sawdust like himself, and he understood that sawdust was quite out-of-date and should never be mentioned in modern circles. Even Timothy, the jointed wooden lion, who was made by the disabled soldiers, and should have had broader views, put on airs and pretended he was connected with Government. Between them all the poor little Rabbit was made to feel himself very insignificant and commonplace, and the only person who was kind to him at all was the Skin Horse.

The Skin Horse had lived longer in the nursery than any of the others. He was so old that his brown coat was bald in patches and showed the seams underneath, and most of the hairs in his tail had been pulled out to string bead necklaces. He was wise, for he had seen a long succession of mechanical toys arrive to boast and swagger, and by-and-by break their mainsprings and pass away, and he knew that they were only toys, and would never turn into anything else. For nursery magic is very strange and wonderful, and only those playthings that are old and wise and experienced like the Skin Horse understand all about it.

"What is REAL?" asked the Rabbit one day, when they were lying side by side near the nursery fender, before Nana came to tidy the room. "Does it mean having things that buzz inside you and a stick-out handle?"

"Real isn't how you are made," said the Skin Horse. "It's a thing that happens to you. When a child loves you for a long, long time, not just to play with, but REALLY loves you, then you become Real."

"Does it hurt?" asked the Rabbit.

"Sometimes," said the Skin Horse, for he was always truthful. "When you are Real you don't mind being hurt."

"Does it happen all at once, like being wound up," he asked, "or bit by bit?"

"It doesn't happen all at once," said the Skin Horse. "You become. It takes a long time. That's why it doesn't often happen to people who break easily, or have sharp edges, or who have to be carefully kept. Generally, by the time you are Real, most of your hair has been loved off, and your eyes drop out and you get loose in the joints and very shabby. But these things don't matter at all, because once you are Real you can't be ugly, except to people who don't understand."

"I suppose *you* are Real?" said the Rabbit. And then he wished he had not said it, for he thought the Skin Horse might be sensitive. But the Skin Horse only smiled.

"The Boy's Uncle made me Real," he said. "That was a great many years ago; but once you are Real you can't become unreal again. It lasts for always."

The Rabbit sighed. He thought it would be a long time before this magic called Real happened to him. He longed to become Real, to know what it felt like; and yet the idea of growing shabby and losing his eyes and whiskers was rather sad. He wished that he could become it without these uncomfortable things happening to him.

There was a person called Nana who ruled the nursery. Sometimes she took no notice of the playthings lying about, and sometimes, for no reason whatever, she went swooping about like a great wind and hustled them away in cupboards. She called this "tidying up," and the playthings all hated it, especially the tin ones. The Rabbit didn't mind it so much, for wherever he was thrown he came down soft.

One evening, when the Boy was going to bed, he couldn't find the china dog that always slept with him. Nana was in a hurry, and it was too much trouble to hunt for china dogs at bedtime, so she simply looked about her, and seeing that the toy cupboard door stood open, she made a swoop.

"Here," she said, "take your old Bunny! He'll do to sleep with you!" And she dragged the Rabbit out by one ear, and put him into the Boy's arms.

That night, and for many nights after, the Velveteen Rabbit slept in the Boy's bed. At first he found it rather uncomfortable, for the Boy hugged him very tight, and sometimes he rolled over on him, and sometimes he pushed him so far under the pillow that the Rabbit could scarcely breathe. And he missed, too, those long moonlight hours in the nursery, when all the house was silent, and his talks with the Skin Horse. But very soon he grew to like it, for the Boy used to talk to him, and made nice tunnels for him under the bedclothes that he said were like the burrows the real rabbits lived in. And they had splendid games together, in whispers, when Nana had gone away to her supper and left the night-light burning on the mantelpiece. And when the Boy dropped off to sleep, the Rabbit would snuggle down close under his little warm chin and dream, with the Boy's hands clasped close round him all night long.

And so time went on, and the little Rabbit was very happy — so happy that he never noticed how his beautiful velveteen fur was getting shabbier and shabbier, and his tail coming unsewn, and all the pink rubbed off his nose where the Boy had kissed him.

Spring came, and they had long days in the garden, for wherever the Boy went the Rabbit went, too. He had rides in the wheelbarrow, and picnics on the grass, and lovely fairy huts built for him under the raspberry canes behind the flower border. And once, when the Boy was called away suddenly to go out to tea, the Rabbit was left out on the lawn until long after dusk, and Nana had to come and look for him with the candle because the Boy couldn't go to sleep unless he was there. He was wet through with the dew and quite earthy from diving into the burrows the Boy had made for him in the flower bed, and Nana grumbled as she rubbed him off with a corner of her apron.

"You must have your old Bunny!" she said. "Fancy all that fuss for a toy!"

The Boy sat up in bed and stretched out his hands.

"Give me my Bunny!" he said, "You mustn't say that. He isn't a toy. He's REAL!"

When the little Rabbit heard that, he was happy, for he knew that what the Skin Horse had said was true at last. The nursery magic had happened to him, and he was a toy no longer. He was Real. The Boy himself had said it.

That night he was almost too happy to sleep, and so much love stirred in his little sawdust heart that it almost burst. And into his boot-button eyes, that had long ago lost their polish, there came a look of wisdom and beauty, so that even Nana noticed it next morning when she picked him up, and said, "I declare if that old Bunny hasn't got quite a knowing expression!"

That was a wonderful Summer!

Near the house where they lived there was a wood, and in the long June evenings the Boy liked to go there after tea to play. He took the Velveteen Rabbit with him, and before he wandered off to pick flowers, or play at brigands among the trees, he always made the Rabbit a little nest somewhere among the bracken, where he would be quite cozy, for he was a kind-hearted little boy and he liked Bunny to be comfortable. One evening, while the Rabbit was lying there alone, watching the ants that ran to and fro between his velvet paws in the grass, he saw two strange beings creep out of the tall bracken near him.

They were rabbits like himself, but quite furry and brand-new. They must have been very well made, for their seams didn't show at all, and they changed shape in a queer way when they moved; one minute they were long and thin and the next minute fat and bunchy, instead of always staying the same like he did. Their feet padded softly on the ground, and they crept quite close to him, twitching their noses, while the Rabbit stared hard to see which side the clockwork stuck out, for he knew that people who jump generally have something to wind them up. But he couldn't see it. They were evidently a new kind of rabbit altogether.

They stared at him, and the little Rabbit stared back. And all the time their noses twitched.

"Why don't you get up and play with us?" one of them asked.

"I don't feel like it," said the Rabbit, for he didn't want to explain that he had no clockwork.

"Ho!" said the furry rabbit. "It's as easy as anything." And he gave a big hop sideways and stood on his hind legs.

"I don't believe you can!" he said.

"I can!" said the little Rabbit. "I can jump higher than anything!" He meant when the Boy threw him, but of course he didn't want to say so.

"Can you hop on your hind legs?" asked the furry rabbit.

That was a dreadful question, for the Velveteen Rabbit had no hind legs at all! The back of him was made all in one piece, like a pincushion. He sat still in the bracken, and hoped that the other rabbits wouldn't notice.

"I don't want to!" he said again.

But the wild rabbits have very sharp eyes. And this one stretched out his neck and looked.

"He hasn't got any hind legs!" he called out. "Fancy a rabbit without any hind legs!" And he began to laugh.

"I have!" cried the little Rabbit. "I have got hind legs! I am sitting on them!"

"Then stretch them out and show me, like this!" said the wild rabbit. And he began to whirl round and dance, till the little Rabbit got quite dizzy.

"I don't like dancing," he said. "I'd rather sit still!"

But all the while he was longing to dance, for a funny new tickly feeling ran through him, and he felt he would give anything in the world to be able to jump about like these rabbits did.

The strange rabbit stopped dancing, and came quite close. He came so close this time that his long whiskers brushed the Velveteen Rabbit's ear, and then he wrinkled his nose suddenly and flattened his ears and jumped backward.

"He doesn't smell right!" he exclaimed. "He isn't a rabbit at all! He isn't real!"

"I *am* Real!" said the little Rabbit. "I am Real! The Boy said so!" And he nearly began to cry.

Just then there was a sound of footsteps, and the Boy ran past near them, and with a stamp of feet and a flash of white tails the two strange rabbits disappeared.

"Come back and play with me!" called the little Rabbit. "Oh, do come back! I *know* I am Real!"

But there was no answer, only the little ants ran to and fro, and the bracken swayed gently where the two strangers had passed. The Velveteen Rabbit was all alone.

Oh, dear! he thought. Why did they run away like that? Why couldn't they stop and talk to me?

For a long time he lay very still, watching the bracken, and hoping that they would come back. But they never returned, and presently the sun sank lower and the little white moths fluttered out, and the Boy came and carried him home.

Weeks passed, and the little Rabbit grew very old and shabby, but the Boy loved him just as much. He loved him so hard that he loved all his whiskers off, and the pink lining to his ears turned gray, and his brown spots faded. He even began to lose his shape, and he scarcely looked like a rabbit anymore, except to the Boy. To him he was always beautiful, and that was all that the little Rabbit cared about. He didn't mind how he looked to other people, because the nursery magic had made him Real, and when you are Real, shabbiness doesn't matter.

And then, one day, the Boy was ill.

His face grew very flushed, and he talked in his sleep, and his little body was so hot that it burned the Rabbit when he held him close. Strange people came and went in the nursery, and a light burned all night and through it all the little Velveteen Rabbit lay there, hidden from sight under the bedclothes, and he never stirred, for he was afraid that if they found him someone might take him away, and he knew that the Boy needed him.

It was a long weary time, for the Boy was too ill to play, and the little Rabbit found it rather dull with nothing to do all day long. But he snuggled down patiently, and looked forward to the time when the Boy should be well again, and they would go out in the garden amongst the flowers and the butterflies and play splendid games in the raspberry thicket like they used to. All sorts of delightful things he planned, and while the Boy lay half asleep, he crept up close to the pillow and whispered them in his ear. And presently the fever turned, and the Boy got better. He was able to sit up in bed and look at picture books, while the little Rabbit cuddled close at his side. And one day, they let him get up and dress.

It was a bright, sunny morning, and the windows stood wide open. They had carried the Boy out onto the balcony, wrapped in a shawl, and the little Rabbit lay tangled up among the bedclothes, thinking.

The Boy was going to the seaside tomorrow. Everything was arranged, and now it only remained to carry out the doctor's orders. They talked about it all, while the little Rabbit lay under the bedclothes, with just his head peeping out, and listened.

The room was to be disinfected, and all the books and toys that the Boy had played with in bed must be burnt.

Hurrah! thought the little Rabbit. Tomorrow we shall go to the seaside! For the Boy had often talked of the seaside, and he wanted very much to see the big waves coming in, and the tiny crabs, and the sand castles.

Just then Nana caught sight of him.

"How about his old Bunny?" she asked.

"*That?*" said the doctor. "Why, it's a mass of scarlet fever germs! Burn it at once. What? Nonsense! Get him a new one. He mustn't have that anymore!"

And so the little Rabbit was put into a sack with the old picture books and a lot of rubbish, and carried out to the end of the garden behind the fowl-house. That was a fine place to make a bonfire, only the gardener was too busy just then to attend to it. He had the potatoes to dig and the green peas to gather, but next morning he promised to come quite early and burn the whole lot.

That night the Boy slept in a different bedroom, and he had a new bunny to sleep with him. It was a splendid bunny, all white plush with real glass eyes, but the Boy was too excited to care very much about it. For tomorrow he was going to the seaside, and that in itself was such a wonderful thing that he could think of nothing else.

And while the Boy was asleep, dreaming of the seaside, the little Rabbit lay among the old picture books in the corner behind the fowl-house, and he felt very lonely. The sack had been left untied, and so by wriggling a bit he was able to get his head through the opening and look out. He was shivering a little, for he had always been used to sleeping in a proper bed, and by this time his coat had worn so thin and threadbare from hugging that it was no longer any protection to him. Nearby he could see the thicket of raspberry canes, growing tall and close like a tropical jungle, in whose shadow he had played with the Boy on bygone mornings. He thought of those long sunlit hours in the garden — how happy they were — and a great sadness came over him. He seemed to see them all pass before him, each more beautiful than the other, the fairy huts in the flower bed, the quiet evenings in the wood when he lay in the bracken and the little ants ran over his paws, the wonderful day when he first knew that he was Real. He thought of the Skin Horse, so wise and gentle, and all that he had told him. Of what use was it to be loved and lose one's beauty and become Real if it all ended like this? And a tear, a real tear, trickled down his little shabby velvet nose and fell to the ground.

And then a strange thing happened. For where the tear had fallen, a flower grew out of the ground, a mysterious flower, not at all like any that grew in the garden. It had slender green leaves the color of emeralds, and in the center of the leaves a blossom like a golden cup. It was so beautiful that the little Rabbit forgot to cry, and just lay there watching it. And presently the blossom opened, and out of it there stepped a fairy.

She was quite the loveliest fairy in the whole world. Her dress was of pearl and dewdrops, and there were flowers round her neck and in her hair, and her face was like the most perfect flower of all. And she came close to the little Rabbit and gathered him up in her arms and kissed him on his velveteen nose that was all damp from crying.

"Little Rabbit," she said, "don't you know who I am?"

The Rabbit looked up at her, and it seemed to him that he had seen her face before, but he couldn't think where.

"I am the nursery magic Fairy," she said. "I take care of all the playthings that the children have loved. When they are old and worn out and the children don't need them anymore, then I come and take them away with me and turn them into Real."

"Wasn't I Real before?" asked the little Rabbit.

"You were Real to the Boy," the Fairy said, "because he loved you. Now you shall be Real to everyone."

And she held the little Rabbit close in her arms and flew with him into the wood.

It was light now, for the moon had risen. All the forest was beautiful, and the fronds of the bracken shone like frosted silver. In the open glade between the tree trunks, the wild rabbits danced with their shadows on the velvet grass, but when they saw the Fairy, they all stopped dancing and stood round in a ring to stare at her.

"I've brought you a new playfellow," the Fairy said. "You must be very kind to him and teach him all he needs to know in Rabbit-land, for he is going to live with you forever and ever!"

And she kissed the little Rabbit again and put him down on the grass.

"Run and play, little Rabbit!" she said.

But the little Rabbit sat quite still for a moment and never moved. For when he saw all the wild rabbits dancing around him he suddenly remembered about his hind legs, and he didn't want them to see that he was made all in one piece. He did not know that when the Fairy kissed him that last time she had changed him altogether. And he might have sat there a long time, too shy to move, if just then something hadn't tickled his nose, and before he thought what he was doing he lifted his hind toe to scratch it.

And he found that he actually had hind legs! Instead of dingy velveteen he had brown fur, soft and shiny, his ears twitched by themselves, and his whiskers were so long that they brushed the grass. He gave one leap and the joy of using those hind legs was so great that he went springing about the turf on them, jumping sideways and whirling round as the others did, and he grew so excited that when at last he did stop to look for the Fairy she had gone.

He was a Real Rabbit at last, at home with the other rabbits.

Autumn passed and Winter, and in the Spring, when the days grew warm and sunny, the Boy went out to play in the wood behind the house. And while he was playing, two rabbits crept out from the bracken and peeped at him. One of them was brown all over, but the other had strange markings under his fur, as though long ago he had been spotted, and the spots still showed through. And about his little soft nose and his round black eyes there was something familiar, so that the Boy thought to himself: Why, he looks just like my old Bunny that was lost when I had scarlet fever!

But he never knew that it really was his own Bunny, come back to look at the child who had first helped him to be Real.

Acknowledgments

*Grateful acknowledgment is made to the following authors, agents,
and publishers for permission to reprint the stories listed below.*

Beverly Cleary:
"Henry and Ribs" from *Henry Huggins,* by Beverly Cleary. Copyright 1950 by William Morrow and Company, Inc. Renewed in 1978 by Beverly Cleary. Reprinted by permission of Morrow Junior Books, a division of William Morrow & Company, Inc.

Harold Courlander:
"Talk" from *The Cow-Tail Switch and Other West African Stories,* by Harold Courlander and George Herzog. Copyright © 1975 by Harold Courlander. Reprinted by permission of Henry Holt and Co., Inc.

Joan Tarcher Durden:
"The Cat That Could Fly" copyright © 1994 by Joan Tarcher Durden. Reprinted by permission of the author.

Johanna Hurwitz:
"The Report Card" from *Russell Sprouts,* by Johanna Hurwitz. Copyright © 1987 by Johanna Hurwitz. Reprinted by permission of Morrow Junior Books, a division of WIlliam Morrow & Company, Inc.

Astrid Lindgren:
"Pippi Goes to the Circus" from *Pippi Longstocking,* by Astrid Lindgren, translated by Florence Lamborn. Copyright 1950 by the Viking Press, Inc., renewed © 1978 by Viking Penguin Inc. Reprinted by permission of Viking Penguin, a division of Penguin Books USA Inc.

Alice Low:
Herbert's Treasure copyright © 1971 by Alice Low. Reprinted by permission of the author.

Margaret Mahy:
"The King's Toys" from *Tick Tock Tales,* by Margaret Mahy. Copyright © 1993 by Margaret Mahy. Reprinted by permission of J. M. Dent Publishers, a division of The Orion Publishing Group Ltd.

Nicholasa Mohr:
Text of chapters 4 and 5 from *The Magic Shell,* by Nicholasa Mohr. Copyright © 1995 by Nicholasa Mohr. Reprinted by permission of Scholastic, Inc.

James Riordan:
"The Wonderful Pearl" from *The Woman in the Moon and Other Tales,* by James Riordan. Copyright © 1984 by James Riordan. Reprinted by permission of Dial Books for Young Readers, a division of Penguin Books USA Inc., and by Hutchinson Children's Books, an imprint of Random House UK Ltd.